WHEN HAPPINESS CAME DOWN FROM *HEAVEN*

Written by

CURT YOUNG & FRANK SNYDER

When Happiness Came Down from *Heaven*

Written by Curt Young and Frank Snyder

Acknowledgements

Thank you to our friends in the Authors Guild of Tennessee Writers' group for their encouragement, support, and guidance, supplying us with suggested edits as we wrote When Happiness Came Down From Heaven.

Thank you to Sammy Millan for formatting the book, completing the cover, and adding the short book description on the back cover.

A special thank you to Deana Charcalla-Bean for her patience and guidance in getting the book published on Amazon. Her talent and understanding are a blessing for all wood-be authors.

Curt and Frank would like to thank our former high school classmates for the time we enjoyed together and the experiences that happened during our high school days.

Finally, we would like to thank Shay Young for her expertise in bringing the cover of our book exactly to the way we envisioned it.

Prologue

Diane screamed, "Mary, watch out!" The baseball was hit with a mighty force and the sound of the strike ricocheted around the ballpark as if a train was colliding with a rock wall. Fans heard the echoes of cracking bones. Gasps of shock were everywhere. Mary lay there motionless as Diane scrambled to help. "Mary, Mary, answer me!" Diane frantically checked Mary to see if she was breathing. "Please let me know you're okay!" But there was no movement. No reply. Mary was motionless and out cold.

First aid responders were at the scene immediately as the game came to a screeching halt. Fans around the poor girl did not move, hoping and praying for the best result.

The batter stood at home plate in disbelief. The netting around the first baseline was in place to stop the ball, but it hadn't.

Mary lay there, long gone into deep subconsciousness. Where had she been, and what was she doing? "Mom, why have you done this to me? If you loved Dad, how can you now love someone else? You started dating another guy when I was at Mama Cossitt's for the summer. I don't understand. Does the flag you received at the funeral mean anything? Mama, please help me! My mind is going crazy! What is happening?"

"Calm down, young lady," stated Mama Cossitt. "Let's continue practicing your piano and singing that superb song you wrote."

Chapter 1

MARY

On a beautiful Sunday morning in late summer of 1963, Mary sat next to Mama Cossitt, turning the pages of the songbook as her Mama played the spiritual hymn "It Is Well with My Soul." People sang along with the well-tuned piano, creating an atmosphere of holiness and worship. The preacher sang loudly even though the notes he hit were sometimes off-key and sounded like a bass drum with a hole in it. No one cared because that wasn't why they were there. Pastor Bill's sermon, "Eve Ate the Peach," was posted on the marquee at Ebenezer Church, located in Cotton Plant, Mississippi. People's curiosity had their minds swirling.

The special music was next. With Mama Cossitt's encouragement, Mary sang their family's favorite song, "Amazing Grace". Her three cousins, Mildred, Helen, and Johnnie, were her backup harmonizers. Mama and Papa Cossitt had talked her into singing as a favor to them, as this was her last Sunday with them before returning home to Caledonia, Mississippi.

As the preacher introduced Mary and her song, she left her seat next to her Mama, hugged her, and headed up to the altar. Looking over the congregation, she suddenly felt a peace surrounding her. Her confidence was growing more and more each time she sang. Mama started playing as Mary's voice produced the most wonderful sound ever heard in that sanctuary of the old farm community church. Everyone was completely silent, listening to Mary sing her beautiful rendition of the song. People did not want it to end as she was fabulous. Mama Cossitt had often told Mary that her four-octave voice range was a special gift from God.

The highly anticipated sermon had taken second fiddle to Mary's song, and the preacher knew it. The preacher explained in his sermon in detail how nowhere in the Bible did God say that the fruit was a peach or even an apple. It was only the fruit of the Tree of Life and the Tree of Knowledge of good and evil. The sermon was interesting, but people that day would remember Mary's song more than anything else they heard.

After the service had ended, people expressed to Mary how much they enjoyed her wonderful song. Even Pastor Bill praised Mary, saying, "You should become a professional singer. Your voice and the way you sang that song gave me goosebumps all over my body. Please come back and sing for us again."

Mary replied, "Thank you, pastor, I will. I am glad the peach wasn't the bad fruit, or I could never eat my Mama's peach cobbler again."

Later that day, Mary wrote in her diary about all the compliments she had received, and her thoughts on becoming a professional singer might not be such a bad idea. "I need to talk about this with someone who can understand me. Maybe I will write to my cousin, Diane, and see what she thinks. Diane is very talented as a musician; she might be able to give me some ideas on how to proceed."

The summer was drawing to a close. Returning to Caledonia High School for her junior year was about to happen. Mary now had a plan for her future, and she was excited. She wanted to make her mother proud and hoped she would support her in this journey. Mary also wanted to become someone special like her deceased father. Writing in her diary, she highlighted her phrase, "I MISS YOU AND WILL ALWAYS LOVE YOU, DADDY." He was a soldier during the Korean conflict and never returned.

Chapter 2

DIANE, BOB, & KRIS

Diane left her last-period history class and headed toward the student lockers. It had been a long day, and she was ready to meet with her great friends, Bob and Kris. It was Friday, the end of a tiresome week of junior classes, with a fun weekend to look forward to. The three of them, called the odd plus-one couple, had planned to go shopping, see a movie, eat at their favorite hangout, and then finish the evening doing what juniors like best- nothing. At least that is what their parents said.

They attended Riverwood High School in a small North Dakota community called Riverwood. The population was fewer than two thousand people. This gave the students many advantages over larger schools: The students could participate in any activity they desired without fear of much competition from other students.

Diane rounded the corner near her locker as Bob left his public speaking class. "Bob," she called out, "are you ready to see the movie `**LOVE STORY**`?"

"Absolutely," he responded, eager to leave the building. "I hope Kris can get away from his workout routine. The coach wasn't in a good mood this afternoon when I saw him, but hopefully, Kris can smooth it over and sneak away without punishment. You know how coaches are who have to win all the time."

"Look, here he comes now," Diane informed him as she looked down the hall toward the gymnasium. "He doesn't seem too happy, so I hope everything is okay. Hey Kris," she said as he approached her and Bob, "How is our favorite athlete today?"

"A bit tired and confused," he replied. "Coach was so wishy-washy about our workout today that I finally snuck out when he wasn't paying attention. He's so fixated on getting us ready for the baseball season that I think he loses touch with reality sometimes. Anyway, I'm here and ready to go."

"Don't say that, Kris!" scolded Diane. "He's a great coach and wants the best for you and the whole school. Now tell us, did he say you could leave?"

"Yes, he did. I'm just kidding. He said to have a great time, but to be ready for practice tomorrow afternoon. Let's go!"

The three of them headed out of the school to Kris's jacked-up Volkswagen Beetle parked along the sidewalk. Kris put oversized tires on the back of the bug so that if they ever got stuck in the snow in North Dakota, they could get out of the vehicle, pick it up, move it to a clear area, and drive off. It made sense to him anyway.

The odd plus-one couple was just as it seemed. Diane, a student of the arts, focused on music. She could play any song on the piano, sing along with the music with her beautiful soprano voice, and entertain people of any age with a personality that would flabbergast anyone present. Bob, on the other hand, had the gift of gab. He was into public speaking, debate class, or arguing with every person he didn't agree with or seemed to disagree with, just for the fun. He would always tell them later that he was kidding and trying to have a good time. Kris was the athlete of the odd group, as you can imagine. He played every sport possible when that sport was in season, sometimes overlapping sports as one had not finished and the next one started.

The odd couple + 1 were together by their willingness to support one another. Bob and Kris were always at Diane's performances, and Diane and whichever fellow was not busy were at the other guy's activity. It was a bond that no one knew how it started. It didn't matter, but one thing everybody was sure would last a lifetime.

As they drove toward the movie theatre in the next town, Diane was reading a letter she had received from her cousin in Mississippi. "Hey guys, listen to this. My cousin, Mary, wrote informing me that the preacher at their church preached a sermon on Genesis last month. He said Eve caused the first sin by eating a peach, not an apple. He then told them that wasn't the case and only wanted to get their attention. Maybe he said it's a peach because they're next to Georgia. Mary also said she sang a solo and received praise from the audience. She is now considering becoming a professional singer. Wouldn't that be something, both of us into music?"

"Whoopee," exclaimed Kris. "One singer in your family is enough, especially since you are the greatest. Tell us more about the peach."

"Remember our youth director said that nowhere in the Bible does it state what fruit was eaten, only that it was from the tree of good and evil," Bob announced. "I looked it up, and the fruit that Eve ate was never mentioned. So, we can decide what we think it was."

"Let it go, debate man," Kris suggested. "But it would be fun to find out what everyone thinks. Many questions about the Bible need to be answered, not just that one. Maybe she will provide us with more interesting stuff in the future."

Diane, listening intently, replied, "I don't know, but I would sure like for you two young men to meet Mary someday. I just met her at our last family reunion and hope to see her again this summer at our next get-together. I know both of you would love her."

"Does she like baseball?" Kris asked.

"Cool your jets," Bob replied. "Anyway, the theater is right over there. I have much to say about the question, Kris, but we don't have the time right now."

Diane interrupted them. "Now, my two handsome gentlemen, let's not argue but have a good time."

"By the way, what is the name of the movie?" Kris said.

* * * * * * * * * * * * * * * *

A few hours later, Kris maneuvered the car out of the movie theater parking lot as they headed toward the local burger joint. Bob was the first to talk. "It's so sad she died, and his dad was a jerk for not helping them."

"Let it go and just say it was a good movie," replied Diane. "I was especially impressed by the saying that LOVE MEANS YOU NEVER HAVE TO SAY YOU'RE SORRY. How about you, Kris?"

"It was okay for a movie, but now I'm hungry. If we hurry, we might get to the burger joint in time to watch the rest of the ballgame between the Yankees and the Dodgers."

"Are sports all you think about? Maybe you should try to read a documentary sometime and improve your mind." Bob sounded off. "Try broadening your horizon."

"Now, stop, guys, let's all get along and stick together. There's no place for us to argue. How about I write Mary and see if she can join us in North Dakota sometime? We can see if her pastor has any other comments about the Bible that we can try to figure out for her. How about the question--how many animals did Noah take on the Ark?"

Both boys wrinkled their noses in unison. Bob said, "Let's not go there. We have other things to do besides worrying about animals on an ark or what fruit Eve ate."

Kris remarked, "Let's have some fun together. Go ahead and write her, but we have all we need to take on this world and enjoy what we have."

Diane nodded in agreement. But still, she knew in her heart that it would be better if there were four of them because someday, she would have to choose between them, and she was not ready to do that. They all had their futures ahead of them. All three had two years of high school and college, and then what? Only time will tell.

Chapter 3

MARY HOME

The sun shone brightly on Mary's face while tears rolled down her cheeks. She was standing on the front porch of her mother's home in Caledonia, Mississippi. In one hand, she held a suitcase. Her other hand was waving goodbye to Mama and Papa Cossitt as they drove down the gravel driveway heading back to their country home in Cotton Plant, Mississippi.

The time Mary spent on the farm with Mama and Papa had been too short. It had been enjoyable, and she had learned many new things about music, singing, playing musical instruments, and writing musical arrangements. Mama Cossitt had a music major from Blue Mountain College and was well qualified. These memories Mary would never forget. Mary thought of it as reading an exciting storybook. She had obtained knowledge far beyond her expectations. Now the summer was over, and it was time for her junior year in high school to begin. Mary watched as the old blue and white Chevrolet drove out of sight. She turned toward the front door, reached under the welcome mat to retrieve the key, and opened the door.

Mary entered the small two-bedroom house. She saw the picture of her father and the American flag on the corner cabinet. Next to it was the old piano that Mama Cossitt had given her. "I must sit down on the bench and play it again." But she didn't stop and continued to her bedroom, lifting her suitcase onto the bed. She then headed to the kitchen to retrieve a grape soda pop from the icebox, knowing that her mother would have her favorite drink waiting for her. It was so quiet in the house that Mary just sat at the kitchen table, drinking her soda, wondering what to do next. She rose from her chair after hearing a commotion at the front door. Mary looked around the corner of the kitchen.

Mary's mother, Gale, entered the house, saw her, and yelled, "My little girl is back home!"

Mary ran to her mother, giving her a big hug while crying, "Oh, how I have missed you!"

They both acted like they had not seen each other in years when it had only been June and July. They each started asking the other all kinds of questions. It lasted only a few minutes as Gale glanced at the wall clock. They had two months to catch up on what had happened, but now was not the right time.

Gale looked at Mary sadly, "I'm sorry, but I must hurry. We can continue our conversation when I return from work. I need to change clothes and get to my second job."

Gale left Mary sitting on the couch as she headed to the bedroom to change into her other work clothes. She worked as a waitress at the Ember and Elm Restaurant during the day and as a lobby clerk during the evening at the Fire Tower Falls truck stop and motel. She worked fourteen hours a day on most days.

Several times, Mary asked her mother why she worked so hard and for so many hours. Gale had told her they needed the two jobs to pay for the necessities to survive. Unfortunately, Mary didn't see her mother often because she was always working.

Mary asked her mother about her father many times. The only answer she received was, "he went to war overseas and never returned. He was killed in action, and his body was never recovered." The military told Gale that it was all they could say to her. Mary's only memory of her father was the picture of him in his uniform just before he left for overseas. The picture stood next to the American flag, sitting on the corner cabinet in the living room. Her mother wouldn't say anymore. "Please, let's talk about something else."

Quickly, Gale left the house heading for her second job. Mary waved goodbye, and they agreed to discuss what had happened during the summer later that evening.

Mary was alone again. She looked around for something to do when she noticed the local newspaper sitting on the kitchen table. Reading the paper and catching up on the local news would help her pass the time. Turning to the entertainment section, she suddenly felt like an imaginary person had slapped her face. It was one of those blessings of a wake-up call, as Papa Cossitt would say. Mary got excited as an idea formed in her brain. The article in the newspaper talked about a Music Contest that would be held in downtown Caledonia. She decided to write a special song for her mother and sing it in the Caledonia Community Musical Contest. The goal from the beginning was to show a unique love and bond for her mother using deep emotions. The song had to thank her mother for life, love, and all she did for me. It would be a song applicable to loving daughters and mothers everywhere.

Every year, the local merchants put up prize money for the contest. The leader of the merchant group was a Christian man named Walter. He was a lifelong resident of Caledonia and owned the Big Bear Plunge Dine and Dance Restaurant on Highway 45. If Mary won the contest, she would earn a good-sized financial reward. The prize also included an opportunity to perform at

Walter's Dance Ballroom. Mary immediately started working, writing creatively, formulating words and music for her winning song.

* * * * * * * * * * * * * * * *

Mary stood on the auditorium stage receiving her first-place award three weeks later. She beamed excitedly. She had accomplished what she had dreamed. Gale had learned that the song was for her. She had inspired Mary with her love and devotion shown over the years. What a loving and blessed tribute to Gale.

After the talent contest, Mary formed an all-girls band that played at Walter's Dance Ballroom every Friday night. The local high school students enjoyed dancing and listening to the music. Even students from area schools regularly attended, making Walter's the hot place to go. Mary and her band became very popular. Walter bragged about them by saying it had been the best thing to happen to him and his business. What a ride it had become.

Mary's dream had been accomplished. Winning the contest made it possible to help her mother financially, which she did. The money she earned on Friday nights helped her purchase an airplane ticket to North Dakota to see her cousin, Diane. The trip was scheduled during their spring break. Mary was ecstatic about the future experience.

Mary remembered Mama Cossitt saying, "It is a great day to be alive, with all the wonderful things happening."

Chapter 4

SPRING BREAK

The Caledonia High School Spring Break had arrived. Mary had her plane ticket and was heading to North Dakota. She was excited to spend a few days with Diane, her best friend and closest family cousin.

Diane had mailed several letters to Mary about the events she had planned during their school spring break. Each day had been arranged, and she was not to worry about anything. A special surprise was also being worked on, so just come and have fun.

Mary wondered if the surprise would be a blind date with some handsome guy. She was excited about that possibility and tried to imagine what it would be like. Being slightly larger than most girls her age, she hadn't been on a date with a young man, and her figure had not fully developed like her mother's. Mary would often tell her mother that her figure was the envy of every woman.

The airplane landed at Bismarck Airport, and Mary disembarked, running through the terminal looking for Diane. Suddenly, a screaming girl appeared. It was Diane. They ran to each other as both girls hugged and asked questions simultaneously. All the surrounding people looked in awe at the hysterical young ladies. The cousins were together again with high expectations for the days to come.

After retrieving Mary's luggage, they took off in Diane's car heading toward the small town of Riverwood, North Dakota. Diane kept congratulating Mary on her success in winning the musical contest back home, thus being able to travel north to visit her. She had a hard time waiting to tell Mary what plans she had been working on regarding their future education in college after high school. The timing wasn't right at this point. That would come a few days later in the week.

Diane explained to Mary what they would do daily, but not in detail. One thing Diane said that confused Mary was their venture after high school graduation. Diane wanted to attend college. At one time, Mary had the same expectations. The question that kept haunting her was the cost. Diane seemed to have no concern about the cost of college. Mary never considered the problem until her mother mentioned that working two jobs covered the necessities for them to live. College was not a necessity. Maybe she needed to forget college and focus on making money by singing in a band. What would college offer her was a question that had no answer. Playing in a band and singing was a source of income. She dreamt that a hit song would make her lots of money.

Diane interrupted Mary's thoughts by suggesting they stop to eat at The Pizza at the Cove. "They have the best pizza and milkshakes of anybody in the state."

After eating, Diane and Mary visited the Lewis and Clark Interpretive Center along the Missouri River north of Bismarck. "This is where Lewis and Clark spent a winter on their trek westward toward the Pacific Ocean while exploring the Louisiana Territory," Diane explained.

Mary looked at all the informative displays. She was amazed by all the rough tools she saw and the canoes hollowed out of trees to make them into boats for travel. On the wall was an explanation display showing their traveled route led by their guide, Sacagawea, a 16-year-old Shoshone woman.

Next, the girls stopped at the actual wooden fort. It seemed small to Mary, but it provided shelter to the Lewis and Clark party during the winter of 1804 to the spring of 1805. This was exciting and interesting to Mary.

The next day was supposed to have been when the big surprise for Mary was to have taken place. It was ruined by a sudden decision by the baseball coach at

Riverwood High to take the team on a five-day training camp. The coach had recently gotten approval from the school board, so Kris had left town with the other players to attend the baseball camp.

Diane had hoped that the four of them, Bob, Kris, Mary, and she, would go on a double date to the movies, followed by attending a dance. She didn't know which two couples would be together, but decided they could switch back and forth, changing partners as they wished. Bob took the three of them anyway, having a great time since he had never been out with two beautiful ladies together. Mary had numerous guys ask her to dance during the evening, giving her a wonderful time. This allowed Diane and Bob an opportunity to pursue a relationship, which resulted in their first real bond with each other. Call it a turning point in their feelings for each other. There was no mistaking what had happened, but now they had to tell Kris. How would they be able to explain it?

The rest of the week flew by with the girls spending time out on Lake Sacagawea, riding in a pontoon boat, and looking at all the beautiful scenery. The lake was ten miles wide at one point, but you could still see from one shore to the other. During their ride, they talked back and forth about girl things and what they liked to do. It was too cold yet to swim in the lake, so they enjoyed each other's company, gabbing about their years in high school and what they had accomplished. Also, what would the future hold?

On Wednesday evening, the church's youth group leader had asked the girls if they would provide the special music for the church service. Diane and Mary hesitated at first, but then decided it was a great opportunity for them to show what they could do.

Their performance was outstanding. They sang a beautiful rendition of "I'll Fly Away," written by Albert Brumley. The girls were ecstatic, which proved to themselves they had a future in music that must be explored.

On Thursday, Diane decided to approach Mary about her plans, or hopefully, both of their plans for the future. Diane didn't beat around the bush, stating, "Mary, you have a beautiful voice and play the piano extremely well. I love singing with you, and we both are equally talented. The music department at the University of Tennessee in Knoxville is outstanding. We should apply to go there and strive to acquire a degree in music. Wouldn't that be great? Think of all the wonderful times we could have together."

Mary emphatically responded, "Yes, it would be great, but you are talking far beyond reality. I have no money. My mother works two jobs now to get by. I play in a band to try to help her out financially. There is no way it would work! I'm sorry."

Diane held up two sets of papers she had received from the university. "Here are scholarship papers we need to fill out and send to the university along with a copy of the recording from last night's song, the copy of your winning song from Caledonia you sent me, and a copy of the song I sang at the music contest in Bismarck last week. I received the highest rating possible in my division. These papers are for a full ride to the university with all expenses paid. God can do miraculous things, so why not give it a shot?"

Mary was stunned. Could they achieve a full-ride scholarship? "Why not give it a try!" she exclaimed as they both proceeded to fill out the papers, which lasted most of the day.

That evening, they met Bob at the local Dairy Queen for a marshmallow butterscotch sundae and told him about their plans. Bob was overjoyed for them, but knew he had to talk to Diane about his feelings for her and what this meant for them.

Mary left the next morning on her flight back to Mississippi, but not before hugging Bob and Diane and making them promise to stay in touch. "Wish I could have met Kris. Hopefully, we will see each other soon," she called out on her way to the departure gate.

"You can bank on it, Mary. See you in Knoxville in the fall." Yelled Diane.

Mary replied, "Hopefully yes. Thanks for the great time and all the great stories of your high school years."

Chapter 5

DIANE

Diane was amazed at everything Mary was involved in within the community. Mary's visit had produced a wonderful time, making both girls very close. Their actions and love resembled each other's, so they knew their future meant spending more time together. Applying for scholarships at the University of Tennessee was fantastic, especially if Mary and she were accepted.

Diane thought about what she had been doing the last four years and wondered if her life was as exciting as Mary's. Bob, Kris, and she were involved with the local church youth group. They had participated in local fundraisers. They went on church outings and even traveled to Mexico for a week-long mission outreach in a church-associated orphanage, helping children from newborns to fifteen-year-olds. The odd couple plus one helped rebuild a soccer field, fixed playground equipment, painted walls, and dug a well. They had great fun doing all this, besides showing their love for the children.

Diane's love for music had continued to grow. She played the piano and sang solos during the Sunday morning worship service. She and some other youth group members tried to organize a praise band, but could never get that going because Bob and Kris had voices like door knockers and would not help them.

During Diane's freshman year in high school, she played the piano in a competition and earned a gold star for her performance. That was the highest score one could achieve. She was also in the school choir. During their performance at the state level, she sang a solo on one of the song verses, resulting in the choir receiving an outstanding rating of five stars. All this made her want to pursue music as a career. Diane's love for music was like a volcano growing bigger and stronger as the years passed, just waiting for it to erupt, gushing out of the ground like a geyser.

Bob and Kris were in awe of Diane's development and encouraged her in every situation, except for a praise band. They could not sing or even carry a tune, but showed up at all her performances, supporting her like brothers, showering her with praise and admiration. Even as early as their freshman year in high school, one could tell that both boys had a crush on their favorite young lady.

Diane realized that and hoped it would not become a problem. She loved them in her special way, trying to keep it even between them so it would always be the three of them forever. "Is that possible?" she thought. I don't want to be put in a position where I must choose between them.

The educational part of school didn't seem to go quite as well for Diane as the music. She struggled with history and math. The boys would always try to help, resulting in Bob and her being sent to the principal's office one day. It all started with a week-ending math test. There was a problem she did not understand. She leaned over to Bob and whispered, "Are we trying to figure out the miles between the two places or the time it would take to get there?"

Bob started to reply when the teacher spoke up. "Diane, what are you asking Bob about? Would you like to share that with the rest of the class, or is it private? You know you are not allowed to speak during a test! Some people might call that cheating. Do you have an answer for me?"

Bob, trying to defend Diane, spoke up. "She didn't understand the question, and quite frankly, I don't either."

"Why don't you both ask the principal what the question means, since neither of you thought to ask me?" he replied. "Or did you both just forget the rules about taking a test, which, if I have to remind you, is not talking? Bring me your papers and see if Principal Thompson understands. Don't forget to bring me your permission slips when you return."

The principal, who was also very active in the church youth group, was surprised by who the teacher had sent to his office. "What are you two doing here on a Friday afternoon?"

"I asked Bob a question during a test because I didn't understand what we were trying to figure out, and I still don't," replied Diane. "The teacher saw me."

Bob spoke up, taking the blame, "So we both were sent to your office. I'm sorry and embarrassed, but Diane should not be in trouble."

"You know there is no talking during a test," Principal Thompson sternly replied. "I'm disappointed in both of you. Here are your permission slips to return to class. I'll investigate this situation and see if further punishment is warranted."

Diane and Bob swore this situation would never happen again. Diane was impressed by Bob standing up for her and never complaining about what had happened. This was the first time she remembered having special feelings for Bob.

The final punishment never happened because when the principal investigated the occurrence, he couldn't understand the question, nor could any of the other students. The teacher realized his mistake and gave everyone a correct score for that question. Diane and Bob retook the test with no deductions to their grades.

Probably the most important accolade Diane received during high school was being asked to sing a solo during graduation ceremonies. The song she sang was the same one she had sung in the competition and had received the highest rating possible. The honor was magnified by the fact that she had recently received a full-ride scholarship to attend the University of Tennessee College of Music to further her education. Hopefully, she would be joining Mary, who had also applied for the scholarship to Tennessee. Diane had not heard from Mary but was praying very hard. The members of her graduating class had also voted her the most likely to succeed in life. What an achievement for someone who disliked math and history but loved the arts.

During the commencement ceremony, she kept thinking about Bob and Kris and what they had been through together, what had been accomplished in the last four years, and what the future held for them.

Chapter 6

BOB

The orator of the Odd + 1 couple had the unique ability to talk to anyone. He could take a situation and turn it around in his favor with the gift of gab. Bob loved getting together with Diane and Kris to spend time with "normal people", as he called them. He never felt like he had to prove anything, and could just be himself with them.

Bob was brilliant. He could read an article and retain everything he had just learned. Some of his classmates called him a freak, but never Diane and Kris, which is why he got along with them so well. They always had his back, and he had theirs.

Mary's visit with Diane was a wonderful time for him. In his eyes, Mary was a beautiful lady, just like Diane. Bob had enjoyed their company, helping Diane show Mary the sites in the town of Riverwood. The only bad thing was that Kris was away at a baseball camp, so he hadn't had an opportunity to meet Mary. Bob envisioned the four of them together, but unfortunately, it hadn't happened. His relationship with Diane grew closer during this time. He realized he had developed special feelings for her.

Bob excelled in debate clubs, academic competitions, and language achievements. He could speak Spanish, French, and German, besides English. He was never pushy and didn't let any of this knowledge go to his head. He didn't brag, he just wanted to be part of the group. It was hard at times, as only Diane and Kris understood him. While the others in the class seemed to avoid him, they recognized his intelligence as a leader.

The only trouble he had gotten into in high school was when he tried to help Diane with a math question, which eventually turned out okay. Otherwise, he stayed away from situations that could lead to trouble. He was always looking toward the future, trying to foresee the outcome before it occurred.

He made it a point to attend all of Diane's and Kris's functions as they came to his. They supported one another to the fullest. Besides, their church youth group gave him many opportunities to grow mentally and spiritually as he grew toward adulthood. This had a significant impact on him.

Bob was honored to be elected president of his freshman and senior classes. In between, he served as the secretary in his sophomore year and vice president in his junior year. Even though he was a fast learner, his classmates valued his knowledge for helping their class excel compared to the other grades. Bob wrote the senior class motto, "Students of today, Leaders of tomorrow".

The debate club proved to be Bob's finest hour during his four years in high school. Each year, the Riverwood debate team won the Missouri River Valley scholar title, competing against sixteen other Class 6A schools in the area. Most of this was due to Bob's knowledge, skill, and humor in critical times during the competition. He could tear up any other person's reasoning and get them so frustrated they could not think of a competent comeback within the time limit allowed. Other schools hated it when they saw on the schedule that Riverwood would be there competing.

Diane and Kris, of course, never missed any of the debates that Bob competed in. They were his best supporters, but not his best critics, because they had no idea where he came up with all his responses or reasoning. They were as mystified as much or more than the competitors. Diane and Kris were very proud as Bob had received a four-foot-tall trophy after each competition, proclaiming him as the most valuable debater, an honor that also went to their school and the reputation that followed.

Bob was encouraged by both the pastor and the youth group leader to speak often in church. This made him nervous, but it never showed. Everyone wondered if this encouragement would impact what he would pursue as a lifelong career. No one knew then what he was thinking or feeling, but they hoped it might influence him.

His feelings toward Diane became apparent as the years of high school passed. Bob worried about how this would affect his relationship with Kris, so he kept it to himself until their senior year, when he built up the courage to ask Diane to attend the prom. Diane was surprised but also excited. Of course, she said she would go, but told Bob that he had to get an okay from Kris. Bob dreaded this worst of all. How would he talk to Kris?

The day Bob finally mentioned the prom to Kris was easier than he had thought. Kris said, "Bob, what is bothering you? You've been on pins and needles for a week now. It's time to get it off your chest. Out with what is going on!"

Bob just blurted it out. "I've asked Diane to go to the prom with me, is that okay?"

Kris looked at Bob with a startled look, which then changed to a smile. "I thought this might happen. You are sweet on our best friend, aren't you? You son of a gun. You got up the courage to ask her before I could. You deserve to take her, but only on one condition. You must agree to let me have at least one dance with her during the night, or no blessing."

Bob replied, "Sure thing, but we both know that Diane will insist on more than one dance with you. So, are we still okay and best buds?"

"Absolutely." Now I need to get busy finding someone to take to the prom. Maybe I'll call Farrah Fawcett. Do you think that would be possible? I'm sure she has followed my whole career in high school!" Kris replied sarcastically.

Bob laughed hysterically.

Chapter 7

KRIS

The athlete of the odd + 1 couple was Kris. He participated in whatever sport was going on and excelled in it. Ever since he was a little boy growing up on a farm just outside of Riverwood, he was active in anything that had to do with a ball, some stick, throwing a rock, or driving all over the yard on a two-wheeled motorcycle. He claimed to be the next Mickey Mantle, Jerry West, Bobby Hull, or Evel Knievel. It didn't matter, he just had to be one of them. His father loved watching him grow and would spend lots of time with him explaining the basics of each sport so that he could perfect his skill to the best of his ability.

Trying to play all sports, work on the farm, and spend time with Diane and Bob proved challenging. Kris would always have to juggle all activities and try to find time for his studies, which often took a back seat.

Bob had often told him, "Kris, if you studied half as much as you play ball, you would be the number one student in our class, bar none."

Unfortunately, Kris never listened. Farming and family were first, followed closely by baseball and his best friends, Diane and Bob. Other things that should have been priorities were seldom in the picture. His parents were frustrated with his grades, but the scores were never bad enough to keep him out of any sport or away from being with his friends. They just knew he could do better. He often told them, "When I get to the majors playing for the New York Yankees, you will be proud of me and my time in perfecting my skills. Just wait and see!"

Kris was disappointed he hadn't met Mary during spring break. He had heard from Diane how beautiful Mary was. Missing a chance for the four of them to do things together was sad. Maybe in the future, he thought, he might get another chance.

Kris's high school years were consumed by his sports activities, Diane and Bob's events, church, and family. There wasn't much time left for anything else. He had many opportunities to date the young ladies in his high school as they swooned over him. He paid no attention to them. All he wanted was to be with Diane and Bob and be on a ballfield, not necessarily in that order. He had special feelings for Diane, but knew that Bob felt the same way.

Kris made the all-conference team in baseball in his junior and senior years. The Most Valuable Player award, the highest batting average, the most hits in a season, and a Golden Glove award for his defensive ability were other awards he received.

One game that stood out more than any other happened in his final season in the championship playoffs. Winning this ballgame meant a trip to the state tournament with a chance to achieve something the town of Riverwood had never seen before.

Riverwood was leading three to two in the bottom of the last inning. All they had to do was get three outs, and they would win. The Bellfield Bombers were rated number one in the state and highly favored, so the score surprised some reporters covering the game. Bellfield had the last at-bat and was taking advantage of the situation. Their first two batters had gotten on base with a single and a walk by the Riverwood pitcher. Bellfield had two men on base and nobody out.

Riverwood's coach came out of the dugout and slowly walked to the pitcher's mound to talk to the pitcher. Kris, the second baseman, joined the coach and the other players in the infield at the mound. The catcher also arrived. The coach only said one thing to the pitcher, "I'm hungry. There is a Dairy Queen on the edge of town. I guess it's time for me to buy supper, so let's finish this game and get something to eat. By the way, relax and throw heat. They can't hit your fastball; if they do, your team is behind you. They will make the plays to protect you. Now I can smell that burger and fries. Let's go to work and finish this game."

The whole team seemed relaxed after the coach's visit. Returning to their positions, they were determined to finish the ball game. The next three pitches to Bellfield's batter were all strikes, with one ball hit down the right-field line as a foul. The pitcher threw three more pitches so close to the strike zone that everyone thought the ump would call, "strike three." But it didn't happen. All three were called balls. The situation was tense. The pitcher took a deep breath and threw the next pitch as hard as possible. The batter swung. The loud crack of the bat told everyone what they feared, or what they were hoping for, depending on which team they were rooting for. The ball was hit on a line drive toward right-center field. The pitcher reached out his glove to his left, but it was too late.

At the crack of the bat, the runners on first and second were off and running toward the next base. Kris, playing second base, dove to his right, reached out as far as he could, trying to catch the ball before it got by him. Miraculously, the ball landed in the tip of his glove for the first out. Instinctively, he rolled over and in the same motion flipped the ball toward second base, where the shortstop was waiting for out number two. The base runners had tried to get back to their bases, but to no avail. The shortstop caught the ball, turned, and fired the baseball toward first base, beating the Bellfield runner back. That was the third out. The team had just completed the seldom-seen triple play to end the game.

Riverwood had won and was headed to the state tournament. Everyone was celebrating as the players hugged each other and jumped around like crazy people, throwing their caps and gloves in the air, trying to comprehend what had just happened.

The fans were going wild with excitement. Diane and Bob looked toward second base, watching Kris sitting on his backside, enjoying the celebration.

As the centerfielder reached him on his way to join the rest of the team, he stopped and helped Kris to his feet, shouting, "Get up, you hero, the game's over. We won! We're headed to the state tournament."

Kris joined his teammates, but not before looking over at Diane and Bob with a big smile, shouting, "Thanks for being here."

Kris received a call from the North Dakota State University baseball coach three days after the game, offering him a full-ride scholarship to play for them next season. What a way to end your senior high school year: A championship, a scholarship, and seeing a dream of playing pro ball come that much closer to reality.

What would Diane, her cousin Mary, and Bob do next year? Was their odd + 1 couple over, or were there new chapters to be written? Who knew what would happen?

Chapter 8

MARY'S FUTURE

Mary was lying in bed, crying. Following her recent trip to North Dakota, her whole world had been turned upside down. She had returned home full of exciting information she wanted to share with her mother, her best friend. All the news she had organized on the plane home had been blown away when she was met at the airport by her mother and a strange man by her side. The news she received from her mother had been devastating. While Mary was visiting with Diane, her mother, Gale, had secretly married some man Mary didn't know. Who was he, and where had he come from? She had seen him at school and was told he was the new football coach. There were so many questions going through Mary's mind. Why did she marry this man? Most people have a wedding. They were married by the justice of the peace. Another question bothering her was why her mother had removed her dad's picture and the American flag from the living room cabinet. Where was it and why? Mary cried more as she realized she was no longer number one in her mother's life.

Why did her mother do this to her? She felt alone, with no one caring anymore. Her emotions turned to hate and resentment.

Gale had secretly been dating this man named Lynn for quite a while. He had been hired during the summer as the new football coach for Caledonia High School. Every morning, Lynn would stop at the diner for breakfast where Gale worked. They had become friends. They loved visiting and shared many common interests. While Mary spent the summer with her grandparents, Gale and Lynn enjoyed many dates. They had developed a special chemistry, resulting in the decision to marry while Mary was in North Dakota.

Gale wondered how Mary would react to the marriage. Lynn and she agreed that being married and then telling Mary afterward would be easier than having Mary reject the marriage beforehand, preventing it from occurring. Gale thought Mary would be okay with it after she explained how they wanted a quick and simple wedding. She was wrong.

Later that day, Mary went to her mother after her crying stopped and her emotions had calmed. Gale and Lynn were sitting at the kitchen table. Lynn had gotten Sunday lunch for them. Mary approached her mother, saying, "I love you very much, and that will never change. It's your life to live and do as you see fit. I will soon be graduating from high school and starting my own life. The only important thing to me is that you are happy." Mary bent over and hugged her mother's neck, kissing her cheek. She looked at Lynn and said, "Please love my mother and always keep her happy." Mary left the kitchen and went back to her room.

Gale was pleased with her daughter's reaction. Mary had insinuated by her actions that Lynn was also accepted, but she was not sure. She told herself that time would make everything okay.

Deep down, Mary didn't hate him but was mad because he had taken her mother away. In her thoughts, he would never be accepted.

Mary's thoughts turned toward her future. She no longer wanted to stay in this house with her mother and new husband. He would never be a father to her. She did not know him and did not care to find out anything about him. She decided to leave her mother and the place she used to call home. Mary realized she was no longer her mother's best friend. Lynn had replaced her. She thought about the money she had been making from her band performances. It no longer would go to her mother to help with the "necessities" to survive. The new husband would have to take over that role.

She was eighteen and soon would be graduating from high school. Mary was scheduled to take the ACT this Saturday morning, but decided against it. She would tell everyone she was taking it, but used the opportunity to visit with Walter. He was the person who had given her all-girls band a job performing at his local dance hall. Maybe he could help her like Colonel Tom Parker did for Elvis Presley. He knew people in the music industry, so she would ask him to help her band pursue a musical career. Mary was sure she could become a famous country music singer and songwriter. Surely, he could help her and the band. Making money now was the only thing she could think about.

Mary knew that the sad part about all the decisions she now made went against everything she and Diane had talked about in North Dakota. How could she tell Diane what she had decided to do with her life? Diane would be so upset and disappointed. Mary struggled for a long time that night, trying to think what to say to her cousin, but finally fell asleep thinking about her new future.

Chapter 9

DECISIONS

Meanwhile, back in Riverwood, Kris had received a scholarship to play baseball at North Dakota State University. Also, he wanted to pursue a career in the medical field, thinking about pharmacy or becoming a doctor. He was encouraged by a dentist friend to look into a pharmacy degree while visiting him at the farm on a sunny day shortly after graduation. Kris's father had planned to become a doctor early in his life, but that all changed when Kris's grandfather got sick and Kris's father had to quit school to take over the farm and raise his other siblings. Also, Kris's neighbor, a state senator, had offered to get him into medical school or, if he desired, an appointment to the Air Force Academy in Colorado. It was all getting so complicated to be pulled in different directions that he finally decided to follow his dream of becoming a professional baseball player. He would attend the university, play baseball, and work toward a bachelor's degree in pharmacy if professional baseball didn't work out.

Diane received a scholarship to study and earn a degree in music from the University of Tennessee. She had decided this would be her path for the future.

Meanwhile, hearing from Cousin Mary that she had not gotten the scholarship caused a temporary setback in her plans. Diane wanted them to be together, so she almost decided not to attend college, but Mary convinced her to enroll.

Mary had said, "I'll join you as soon as possible. Please don't put your dreams on hold because of me. We must walk the paths laid out before us, with no regrets and no turning back. We will be together soon, I promise."

Bob had his ideas about the future, but was very secretive about them. Going to the local junior college for a couple of years before entering seminary school had been considered, but was not definite. He desired to develop his relationship with Diane more than anything, so he finally let his feelings be known. He loved Diane, and that was all there was to it. He wanted to be with her, and no one else.

Diane was thrilled to hear this; Kris was not so much. Diane and Bob told each other that their education must come first. They would write letters to each other and see each other as much as possible. A long-distance relationship could work for a few years.

It would also help both of them to know their true feelings for each other as they continue their education in their chosen career path. They promised each other their love would be forever, and eventually they would be together. Marriage would happen as soon as they graduated from college. Bob had gotten down on one knee, proposed, and made it official.

Kris hated Diane and Bob's decision. He felt left out after all these years of being together. It left a bad taste in his mouth, and the more he thought about it, the more upset and angrier he got. He felt like he had been stabbed in the back by supposedly his two best friends in the world.

Bob and Diane, especially Diane, tried to talk to him and explain what had happened, but Kris would have none of it. The rift between them grew deep over the last two weeks before Diane and Kris left for their respective universities. Kris didn't show up for the church youth group or church anymore. He sent Diane and Bob a message from another friend that he never wanted to see or hear from them again.

Kris had loved Diane and Bob. His love for Diane was more than he had ever told anyone about. In Kris's mind, whom did he have to talk to about anything except Diane and Bob? Now he had separated himself from them. This hurt would take a long time to get over, but he was determined to do so. It affected him mentally as well as spiritually.

A couple of future teammates playing baseball at the university contacted him before leaving home, asking him if he wanted to join them for a night out in Bismarck. Normally, he would never have considered this invitation because he knew what they had insinuated, partying with girls with liquor involved. He felt sad and lonely, so "what the heck," he replied, "Let's go have some fun. Maybe I'll meet someone new who will help me forget my problems."

"You know, you might even get lucky," said one of his teammates, "if you know what I mean."

What happened that night brought out a new person in Kris, and not for the better. In one night alone, he learned the ways of the world that would affect him for years to come. Partying, drinking, and learning swear words he had never heard before started to sound natural to him. He realized that some ladies have no respect for themselves, and saw how much fun he could have and not worry about it the next day, even if he remembered what had happened.

Every once in a while, in the back of his mind, he wondered about Diane and Bob, but it never lasted long because they had left him. He had been devastated. Kris left his past behind. His friends, religion, and respect seemed to be gone in a flash, all because two recently graduated high school boys thought they were in love with the same lady. Unfortunately, he had become the odd one out. The lady had chosen the other one.

Chapter 10

SINGING

Mary graduated from Caledonia High School and was determined to become a singer and songwriter. She had written Diane about her decision, which hadn't gone well with Diane. Diane had wanted to know if Mary had applied for the scholarship or even taken her ACT exams. Mary had given her the right answer in her mind, which was no to both questions, but encouraged Diane to achieve the goal for both of them. She had told Diane it was about money, which wasn't a lie.

Walter had agreed to become her business agent. Walter was a Christian at the Independent Caledonia Church. He was also a successful businessman and had contacts and influences in the music industry in Nashville. Mary and Walter were a perfect fit to help her strive to accomplish her goals.

Walter had secretly talked to Mary's mother, Gale, and understood their situation. Gale asked Walter to help Mary, and he agreed to do his best. He promised to stay in touch with her and let her know how her daughter was adjusting to her new life and business career.

Walter, a part-owner of a nearby trailer park called the Creekside, had arranged for Mary and some of her band players to rent a trailer. The rent would be paid from some of the financial proceeds of the girl's Friday night band performances at the dance hall. The band and the Friday night gigs were doing well. This gave Mary time to focus on her songwriting while learning from Walter the proper business management of the band.

Abby was the Band's piano player. She was dating the local newspaper editor's son. This opened the door for some special advertising in the newspaper. It also provided good musical news articles about their band and the players involved.

Many good things were happening in Mary's life. This made her forget the bad times and concentrate on the future and the good things to come.

One day, Mary was in the Big Bear Plunge Dine and Dance Ballroom building, waiting for Walter in his plush office. He had insisted on meeting with her. She sat waiting in a chair across from his mahogany desk. When he arrived, he sat in his oversized leather chair, leaned back, and continued chewing a stogie cigar. Walter had become a special person in Mary's life besides being her music agent. He was her new stepparent. He was everything to Mary and so much more. Mary and Walter had discussed the summertime at Mama Cossitt's house and the Church Rule, which was that you can't work on Sunday. Walter had laughed out loud during that conversation. He leaned forward on his desk, looking directly at Mary, and spoke. "I like the Church Rule and have the same one for my business. We work every day but not on Sunday. That day is set aside for the Lord. You will be in church on Sundays if you are to be a business partner with me. The only exception is if you are sick."

Mary grinned, saying, "Okay."

Walter looked into her eyes and smiled broadly. He knew in his heart what he must do for her. She never had the chance to experience having a father, so now he would change that for her.

Walter began by organizing a team of professionals who would turn Mary into a new person. He thought about the famous people in the music world. Elvis, Liberace, Dolly, and Loretta Lynn, to name a few. They were dressed in the best flashy and flamboyant outfits when they walked out onto the stage in front of their fans and the world. Walter wanted this environment for Mary and the girls in her band. He wanted them to be talked about, but in a Christian way.

His wish for Mary was to become the best singer-songwriter in country music. Along the way, he would do all in his power to explain the pathway to happiness.

Walter always told Mary, "Write songs that control people's emotions. Perform them from your heart and inner soul. This will provide you with a world of musical fans who will dedicate themselves to you for life.

Months passed as Mary's rise to fame began to grow. She had written songs and performed locally at numerous gigs with stunning success. She worked hard with a dedicated work ethic to improve her skills and performance. It was paying off.

Walter walked into the office one day with a broad smile. He had just secured a record contract with Rainbow Records. Mary was on her way toward stardom. He had booked many performances for the group in the months to come. One of the first big gigs would be in late winter or early spring at a joint in St. Petersburg, Florida, called the Tailspin Racer. She was scheduled to perform for three nights.

During their trips to play music, Walter warned them about getting involved with the young men they came in contact with. Be careful and use common sense was preached to the band. "You never know what could happen on these trips. I can't be with you all the time."

Mary's life was on a steady climb upward. God had been so good to her and the band. She was so thankful for all her blessings, but would it last? What was in store ahead?

Chapter 11

Bob and Diane

Bob was sure about what he wanted in life. He had known for a long time that his love for Diane was pure. All through high school, and especially the wonderful nights talking, sharing, and encouraging each other, his passion had grown so much for Diane that he could not help but want to share it with her. The days he sat in the stands holding her hand while watching Kris during his sporting events, or the evenings at church youth group when they shared their feelings about God and their lives in the future, were in his mind. All this had influenced his decision about what he would do now that high school was finished.

"I'm going to attend seminary school this fall at the Cascades Baptist College, Fargo, North Dakota," he told his parents the week after graduation. "I hope you'll accept my decision and support me. I have been thinking about this for a while now, and it just feels like the right thing for me."

Bob's dad, Charles, an electrical engineer, replied, "Are you sure this is right for you? We know of your love for the church and God, and doing His work, but I thought you would follow in my footsteps and become an engineer. Please don't get me wrong, son; we want the best for you."

"I have thought about it a lot, Dad, and I feel this would be the best place where I can help other people and impact their lives. Also, Mom and Dad, I have made another important decision. I plan on talking to Diane's father today about asking his daughter to marry me. Now don't get too excited. This won't happen until we finish our schooling and get our degrees. Diane is a wonderful lady, and I love her very much."

Bob's mother spoke quickly but quietly, "Your dad and I have thought about this happening and have already talked it over. We support you with all our heart. You have found a precious young lady. We know you will be happy. We wish you God's grace. Also, your grandmother's ring is available. She asked me to give it to you when the time was right. Would you like to have the ring to give to Diane?"

"Oh yes, please! I didn't know what I was going to do about that. Thank you both so much. I love you."

Charles just smiled, nodding his head in agreement. Then he said, "We love and support you, son."

Later that evening, Bob was sitting in Diane's father's office waiting for an opportunity to visit with him. Dave, Diane's father, was finishing up his day's work before heading home. When the final report was taken care of, he filed it away and turned his attention to Bob. "Now, young man, you wanted to talk to me. I have a suspicion about what you will say, so let's start, shall we? I've known you for a long time and know you have great expertise in debating; thus, I will listen intently."

Bob didn't beat around the bush as he came directly to the point. "Sir, I have known your daughter for a long time now. We grew up together, went through elementary and high school, enjoyed activities, and participated in youth group events. We have become very close over the last few years. With you and your wife's permission, I would like to ask Diane to marry me."

Dave was taken by surprise. This is not what he thought Bob had on his mind. He looked at Bob, replying, "Hell no! You're both too young. You have just graduated from high school and are only eighteen. Diane is only seventeen. What is the big hurry? Give yourselves some time to see the world."

Bob chuckled as his confidence burst forth. "I don't mean right now. We need our education first and then marry, in say four years. That will give us time to get to know each other fully and see how we act when we are at different universities and states that are not close to each other. Diane will be in Tennessee, and I'll be in North Dakota. We'll have time to plan and explore our wishes and fears for the future. I love her and want her to know that, too."

Dave looked at Bob with a daunting smile. "You always did know what to say, didn't you? I'll discuss this with my wife and see what she says. Don't get your hopes up too high. Diane's Mom is pretty protective."

* * * * * * * * * * * * * * * *

Two days later, Bob got the permission he needed, but with the stipulation that they had to wait until their schooling was completed. He was elated and knew how to carry out his plan in the most romantic way. Next week is Diane's eighteenth birthday.

The evening started with a dozen roses delivered to Diane by a special carrier. She was thrilled, immediately enjoying the wonderful smell before putting them in a glass vase, and hurriedly preparing for her date with Bob. He was to pick her up at four o'clock and had told her to dress for a nice dinner and evening, just the two of them. She felt bad about what had happened with Kris, but loved the closeness between Bob and herself. He was everything to her. It made her realize how much she loved him.

Bob took Diane to a special restaurant that sat high on a bluff overlooking the Missouri River and the valley below. Everything was perfect as they stepped out onto the Big River Pavilion veranda after dinner was over. A beautiful, bright orange sunset appeared over the horizon as the sun set in the west. As they sat down on a loveseat to enjoy the perfect evening, Bob turned to Diane while holding her hands, saying, "You are the most beautiful lady in the world. I wish you the most wonderful birthday and hope all your dreams and wishes come true. You're everything to me."

After saying this, Bob stood up, turned toward Diane, and got down on one knee. Holding his grandmother's ring in his right hand, he asked, "Diane, will you marry me?"

Diane's thoughts went in a million different directions. "Yes, yes, I will," she replied as Bob helped place the ring on her finger. "What about our education and plans that we made? My Mom and Dad will kill me. Oh my gosh, I love you!"

Bob smiled, "I have already talked to your parents and gotten their permission. I promised them we would get our education before saying our I do's. I just wanted you to know how much I love you."

"I love you, too." That was the only reply he needed as they hugged each other during the beautiful sunset evening.

* * * * * * * * * * * * * * * *

A month and a half later, Diane was packed and headed for Tennessee while Bob left the day earlier for Fargo and seminary school. Both had made many plans for their future and already had decided on a wedding date. More needed to be done, but they both knew that would come with time. The sure thing was their love for each other.

Chapter 12

BASEBALL SPRING BREAK

For Kris, it was a sad day in the fall of 1965 as he headed off to the State University in Fargo, North Dakota, to continue his education and baseball career, which he loved.

Diane and Bob, Kris's former high school friends, were engaged but decided to delay their wedding until they finished their degrees. They promised each other their love would grow daily, even though they were apart, attending their chosen universities. Diane wanted to achieve a music degree in voice and piano at the University of Tennessee. Bob was set for seminary school in Fargo, North Dakota, knowing that was what God had planned for his life. He was sure he could change the lives of the people he contacted. Diane and Bob were happy with their plan and ready to tackle the world.

Kris, not so much. He had severed ties with his best friends. He often started to call both of them, but his pride kept him from doing so. "All I want to say is, I love you both and want to be friends again." He just couldn't. Something always stopped him. Pride can be an evil opponent, resulting in heartache if it festers too long. Kris had difficulty accepting what had happened between the three of them and knew something had to change.

Kris's first year of college was challenging as partying, drinking, and chasing girls took over most of his life. Classes didn't seem very important, as his grades showed. He flunked out of pharmacy school and was about to be kicked out of college if it wasn't for the sports program. The coaches kept him out of trouble. They saved him several times because of his ability to play baseball. He excelled as a second baseman on the college baseball team. Few freshmen start in their first year, but Kris achieved this goal. He was rewarded by making the all-conference freshman team with a .357 batting average. He had a fielding percentage of 100 percent as he made no errors in the 56 games he played. He was celebrated by the league but was warned by the coach and athletic director to get his grades up or be kicked off the team.

* * * * * * * * * * * * * * *

Six months later, spring training was about to begin. Kris's grades had risen to an acceptable level as he buckled down and finally did some studying. He realized during the off-season that he was about to lose the one thing that was so important to him: baseball. Kris had grown up, and the threat of being kicked off the team had finally brought him back to reality. He wanted to achieve his dream. He had faced Bob's and Diane's engagement, and the three had broken up. He had accepted it. Kris's life was now under his control. No more all-night parties. No more acceptance of inducements from undesirable people that the coaches had warned the team about. He was a new man.

The team had six games in Florida in late March, so they began practicing in early February. During practices, they became closer as most players returned from the previous year. A companionship between the players made everything fun and exciting as everyone prepared for the season to start.

Their first game against the Florida International College baseball team in St. Petersburg resulted in a slugfest. Each team scored double-digit runs with the final score tied after nine innings. Since it was a practice game and both teams had scored thirteen runs, both coaches decided to call the game even and quit for the day. The players weren't happy, but it had been a long, hot game. The coaches knew they had to work on the pitching, and that would develop as the season progressed.

Their next game was three days away, so the coaches told the players they would have the next day off, as the coaches were taking all twenty-four players to the beach for fun and relaxation. Of course, beach volleyball was first on the list. Diving into the sand for digs, jumping high over the top of the net, spiking the ball back into the sand, and shouting smack talk back and forth between the players was the norm. Game after game was played as the players enjoyed the afternoon. Other players swam in the ocean while some lay on the beach, soaking in the sun.

Kris was playing volleyball when a member of the other team knocked the ball way past the end line. It rolled down the beach and was headed for the ocean. Kris ran after it so fast that he unintentionally ran into a young woman walking along the shoreline, knocking her down and making a big splash in the shallow water. She never saw him coming. Kris, looking at her, exclaimed, "Are you okay? I'm so sorry for hitting you. Let me help you up."

The young lady glared at him. "No, I think you've done enough. I'm soaked." She struggled to get up while shaking off the water and sand from her wet clothes. She looked at Kris's pained expression and felt sorry for him. She said, "I guess it was both our faults. I was deep in thought and wasn't watching where I was going. You were going after the ball and didn't see me. Let's forget it."

As Kris threw the ball back to the group, he shouted, "Find someone to replace me. I need a break." He turned toward the six-foot-six-inch brunette and asked, "Are you sure you're alright?"

She nodded and turned to head back from where she had come, not knowing what else to do.

Kris asked, gently, "What is your name? Why were you so deep in thought? Can I help?"

The young lady turned toward him, replying, "I'm a singer at the local pub, and I was rehearsing the songs I want to sing tonight in my mind." Bashfully, she continued, "I don't usually talk to strangers like this. My agent in Mississippi, Walter, told me to beware of young men on the beach."

Kris laughed, "Our coaches told us to be careful meeting any single ladies on the beach, too. I'm here with my college team. We have a few games around the state, but the coaches gave us a day off." He purposely didn't tell her he was a baseball player, thinking that might turn her off. "Where did you say you were singing?"

She smiled. "Two streets over on Third Avenue at a pub called Tailspin Racer. I start singing at 10 p.m. and the set lasts until 1 o'clock. Maybe you could come and listen. If you would like, I could leave free tickets at the door for you and some of your teammates. You might enjoy the music and seeing my other band members."

"I would love to, but I can't. I'm so sorry, we have a 10 p.m. curfew. Can I walk with you on the beach for a while? I have a couple more hours before we return to the hotel."

"I guess that would be all right." They turned and headed back down the beach in the direction she had come. Small talk started first, but as they walked on, she started humming a song she would sing later that night.

"Is that a song you are humming? It sure is pretty." Kris said. "I'll bet you have a beautiful voice. Can I hear you sing the song?"

Mary blushed, "Thank you, but I'm too embarrassed to sing it here on the beach. If you come to the pub, I'd be glad to. My band will be with me then."

"I'd love to, but we leave for Sarasota tomorrow and have a scheduled practice after we get there," replied Kris. They had walked at least half a mile by this time when they stopped. Kris continued, "You sure are pretty. What is your name? How do I contact you? I would love to see you again and take you out on a date for a meal or a movie."

"Maybe we shouldn't go there," Mary replied. "I don't give out my name until I've met someone twice. I fly back to Mississippi tomorrow, so we will probably never see each other again. You seem like a nice guy. Not many men have said I'm pretty, so thanks for saying that; it makes me feel special. I hope your team does well, but I must go now."

Kris said in a soft voice, "May I do one thing first before you go?" He put his hands on her shoulders while leaning over and kissing her cheek.

Mary was taken by surprise but liked it. She looked directly into his eyes as she leaned forward, kissing him on the lips with a passion that would last forever, or so they both thought. She said, "Bye", as she turned and jogged down the beach.

Kris yelled, "Nice to meet you, and I know we'll see each other again. I meant every word I said and hope you become a famous singer."

Mary smiled and mumbled, "I hope I see you again also. You impress me, making me want to know more about you, but it's not in the cards now."

Kris couldn't hear her. She was gone. Kris kicked himself because he hadn't even learned her name.

Chapter 13

Pro Career

For a long time after Kris left St. Petersburg, heading back to North Dakota after spring training concluded, he thought about the young woman he had met on the beach. "I wish I had gotten her name or received a way to contact her," he told his roommate. "She was pretty and had me tongue-tied. She flustered me. A magnetic attraction drew me to her, and I will probably never see her again. I blew it this time. Somehow, I hope I get another chance.

Kris's college classes during his sophomore year had taken a big turn for the better. He had applied himself and looked forward to going to class. His grades reflected the change—a difference between night and day, which pleased both his parents and the coaching staff.

His baseball results were miraculous. He led his team in batting average, hits, runs, and homers, leading the Northern Conference. Somewhere, he had found power in his bat, resulting in dingers that hadn't happened during his freshman year. The coaches and scouts for the major leagues had been thoroughly impressed. Kris had a tough decision to make. Was it time for him to stay or turn pro? He had played well enough to draw lots of attention. His dream felt like it could become reality sooner rather than later. Was it time for him to leave college and further pursue his dream, or wait a couple more years? He had flunked out of pharmacy school, so that wouldn't hold him back.

It didn't take long for Kris to decide what to do. A baseball scout told him he would probably be drafted in the first or early second round. His decision was made. The lure of big money, recognition, and a lifelong dream made the final decision easy. Kris was going to turn pro.

Kris had tryouts with many teams, but enjoyed meeting the management of the Atlanta Braves the best. He was sure they liked him also. They had the twenty-seventh pick of the first round and knew that was when he would be drafted. We all know that the best-laid plans usually never happen. The Minnesota Twins selected Kris as the twenty-first pick of the first round. He was in shock as he hadn't even tried out for that team or been contacted until his phone rang thirty seconds before the pick was announced. Undoubtedly, Minneapolis was convinced that his college team statistics were enough for them to make him their choice.

In the fall of 1967, Kris began his pro career in the Single-A Farm System in Rochester, Minnesota. He started his pro career with a bang, getting two hits in his first game while driving in three runs. Kris hit his first homer over the left-field fence the following night. The ball traveled a measured distance of 428 feet. He added two singles, resulting in a .500 batting average in just two games. That was enough for the parent team to promote him to their Double-A farm team in Indianapolis.

Diane had read the headlines about Kris tearing up the pitching in the minor leagues. Bob and she had not talked with Kris in two years and thought now would be a great time to break the silence. She called Bob and asked, "What do you think I should do?"

Bob replied, "You should call him. I don't think he'll talk to me, so please let me know how he is. Tell him I miss our friendship and think about him often. I truly wish him much success."

"I'll do that tonight after I know his ballgame is over. I hope he doesn't hang up. I, too, miss his friendship. Are your studies going okay, Bob? I know you've been busy studying Greek. We only have two more years left until our degrees are final. Thank God because I miss you!" sighed Diane.

"Love you also, babe," Bob softly announced as he reluctantly hung up the phone.

Later that evening, Diane dialed the phone number she had found for the Indianapolis baseball team headquarters. The secretary answered on the second ring. Diane asked, "Is there any way I can obtain a phone number for one of your players? He has been a very close friend, and I'm trying to catch up with him."

"What is his name?" came the reply.

"Kris Carlson," Diane said.

"You and every other lady in this city have called asking for his number. I tell you what I will do. You give me your name and phone number, and I will pass it on to him. It's in his court, then, if he calls you back. Is that fair enough?"

"If that is the best you can do, thank you. Please see that he gets it. It's important." Diane pleaded.

At eleven o'clock the next morning, Diane's phone rang as she entered her apartment, returning home from class. She picked up her wall phone as she accidentally dropped some of her coffee on the kitchen table, but she didn't care. She was hoping the call was from Kris. "Hello, this is Diane."

"How are you? I got your message last night after the ballgame. Is everything okay?"

"Now that I hear your voice, all's well," Diane said. "It's been too long. Both Bob and I miss you. You're too important in our lives to let this go on. We miss you and know we can get past all the difficulties."

There was silence on the other end, but only for a second. Kris blurted out, "I miss you both, also. The last two years have killed me."

A short phone call turned into a two-hour reunion. Diane and Kris talked about everything. Diane had to stop at one o'clock because her next class started in fifteen minutes. They both promised to stay in touch, never to let what happened to them happen again. They would talk often and be open and honest about everything.

* * * * * * * * * * * * * *

In the spring of 1968, Kris had been promoted to the major leagues. He was flying high and was the starting second baseman for the Minnesota Twins. He was always looking through their schedule to see if he would get a chance to get away long enough to see Diane and Bob. Their school schedule and his had provided all kinds of problems. One day he was playing in Detroit when he received a letter from Diane stating that her cousin, Mary, had been invited to appear on the Ed Sullivan Show that coming June. The Twins had a three-game set against the New York Ball Club starting the day after the Ed Sullivan Show. Immediately, he called Diane, telling her he had two tickets reserved for them at the ballgame the next day. "I hope you can attend. It would be wonderful to see you and finally to meet your cousin. I am looking forward to June."

Chapter 14

SONG, PERFORMANCE, WATCH OUT

Mary and her band's arranged music performances were sell-outs. They had been a huge success. The band's popularity was becoming a musical phenomenon. It was great for the girls, but also for Walter. He said often, "I have missed my calling. I am a perfect musical agent for these ladies, not a restaurant entrepreneur."

Returning home from one of their gigs was usually a long bus ride, with them arriving early the next morning. During the trip, Mary often thought about her father and wondered why he had joined the military. It had not been mandatory, so why had he done it? Her mother told her many times that he wanted to defend his country. That was all she would say. Why did he lose his life? Why had he left her and her mother? "Why" was the word used in all her questions about her father. She missed him deeply and many times felt so alone.

The bus pulled into a gas station for a scheduled fuel stop. Attached to the station was a restaurant. The driver advised the girls it was time to eat and then be on their way. The girls exited the bus and headed toward the restaurant. Before Mary reached the door, something caught her eye. A huge, beautiful, waving American flag was flapping in the breeze. It astonished her to see it in motion as a spotlight displayed it in all its glory. The colors symbolized the men and women who served their country. It made Mary think of her father and the flag the United States Army gave her mother.

She saw the waving flag as if her father was saying, "I'm proud of you, young lady!" The flag was so beautiful in the gusty breeze. Its beauty was magnified by the red, white, and blue colors and the stars representing all the states.

As Mary stood there in amazement, a song began forming in her mind. She started to hum a tune, adding words to describe the flag. This became a new song. Little did she know that this song would propel Mary into stardom. Mary quickly began jotting it down as she forgot about eating. She could eat later. She had to get this music on paper.

The bus was refueled shortly, and the band members were back on board, ready for the final trek home. That didn't stop Mary from working on her new song, "THE RED, WHITE, and BLUE." She didn't know then, but this song would be fantastic and open the door for her appearance on the Ed Sullivan Show.

Walter went ballistic when Mary and the girls performed this new song for him. He started to cry and jumped for joy. He grabbed and hugged her while exclaiming, "You have written and sung an amazing song. It's wonderful and your ticket to stardom. I need to get this song to Ed Sullivan and see what happens. If I'm not mistaken, Mary, this may get all of you on his show and the road forward that has no limits."

Walter was right. After hearing the new song, Mr. Sullivan contacted Walter immediately. He said, "You are invited to bring this young woman and her band to New York City, all expenses paid. I want them to be my guests and appear on the show as soon as we can make the arrangements. My staff will contact you shortly to work out all the details. Congratulations and see you soon."

After hearing the news from Walter, Mary dialed the phone number of her cousin, Diane. She could hardly wait to tell her all that had occurred. Mary wanted Diane to meet her in New York and attend the show. She said, "Please come because I need you by my side. We can take a few days off afterward and see the sights of New York. It will be fabulous. Something we can do together since it's been so long since we've seen each other."

Diane talked to her professors and explained the opportunity to observe the Ed Sullivan Show. They all thought it was a wonderful learning experience, thus giving her permission. As soon as the time was set, Diane would be on her way.

* * * * * * * * * * * * * * *

Mary felt a chill run up her spine as she walked out onto the stage, as Ed Sullivan introduced her to the packed audience. The chill brought back the memory of her Mama Cossitt and the solo she sang at the country church where it all began. Mary looked toward the piano at the side of the stage, where Diane sat on the piano bench alongside the band, ready to play her song. Mary had asked Diane to do this for her after she got to New York. What a surprise.

Diane returned the surprise by saying she had an outing the next day that would please her. It would be a day she would remember forever.

Mary looked into the audience, imagining Mama and Papa Cossitt sitting in the front row. As Ed finished his introduction, he motioned to Mary to begin. Mary proudly announced, "My song tonight is in remembrance of my father, an Army vet, of whom I am deeply proud."

The song, "The Red, White, and Blue," captivated the crowd. Mary's angelic voice brought tears of joy to Ed and the crowd. No one knew about the people who watched on television, but tears were probably everywhere. The night was a dream come true and would never be forgotten by anyone who attended the performance. Mary looked upward, knowing her father was watching and listening to every word. The standing ovation was so loud and long that the television station had to cut away long before they wanted.

The next day, Walter and the band headed back to Mississippi while Mary and Diane were to spend a few days in the big city taking in the attractions.

Mary reluctantly accepted Diane's invitation to attend the baseball game the next day, saying she wasn't into baseball. Diane assured her she would enjoy it and wanted her to meet a special baseball friend. They found their seats and tried to enjoy the introduction of the players. The problem was that many fans recognized Mary from the night before and wanted her autograph. They also wanted to hear her story. Diane tried to intervene, telling everyone to stop, to give her some peace and let her enjoy the ballgame. The fans would listen for a while, but then, like clockwork, a new group would appear.

Two servicemen were talking to Mary when Diane yelled as she heard the crack of the bat, "Mary, watch out!" Diane screamed as Mary fell to the concrete floor. Her body was lifeless. The ball had struck her in the throat and jaw. The emergency crew immediately took control as fans and the ball players looked on in shock.

Kris was horrified because he was the batter who hit the foul ball. He looked at Diane as she glanced down at him with tears running down her cheeks. The netting was supposed to stop the ball. *Why hadn't it, and what had he done?*

Chapter 15

HOSPITAL VISIT

Kris had a hard time finishing the ballgame. He couldn't keep his head in the game. The coach and all the players could see it in his eyes. He struck out three times in a row and made two errors in the field. All he could think about was the lady in the stands who was hit with the ball. Normally, that doesn't bother him. People get hit with balls at games regularly, but she was right next to Diane. Was it her cousin who got hurt? Diane and Bob will never forgive him, and what about her cousin? Her cousin had just performed on the Ed Sullivan show. She was a star, and how would this affect her career? All these questions kept running through his mind.

Finally, the coach pulled him from the game, sending him to the showers. The coach wasn't understanding and told him, "Get your mind back in the game. You are a professional. Act like one. Accidents happen. Get out of here until you can get over this!"

Kris hurriedly showered and headed home. Sleep was nonexistent as he tossed and turned all night long. What could he do? He decided to go to the hospital and find out who the lady was. Is she okay, and is she Diane's cousin? "Please let her be okay," he thought as he twisted and turned in the sheets, trying to sleep.

The next morning, bright and early, Kris was on his way to the hospital. "Do I stop and get flowers or candy before heading to the room?" "What do I say?" He was so torn up that he almost had two accidents on the way.

The receptionist at the front desk pointed him in the direction of the trauma area where Diane's cousin would be. Before heading to the hospital, Kris had called Diane to find out if the injured woman was her cousin.

Diane said, "Yes, it is, and I will meet you in the waiting area. Visiting hours are not until nine o'clock. My cousin, Mary, is pretty sedated and all bandaged up, so don't be shocked."

Diane greeted Kris with a hug as he entered the waiting room. "Do you want me to go with you to see her, or go yourself?"

Kris responded, "This is something I need to do by myself. I'm so sorry, Diane. I didn't mean for her to get hurt. Can you please forgive me?"

"Bob and I love you, Kris. You don't need to apologize for anything. Freak accidents happen. I hope Mary will be okay. Just tell her she is in good hands and God will take care of her."

"I don't know if I can do that. God and I are not on the same path right now. A lot has happened in the last three years, and most of it has not been good. I'm a different person from the one you knew before. God has not been much of a part of it," a downtrodden Kris replied.

Diane responded, "Bob and I are praying for you. You are not lost; you have just taken the wrong path for a while. Remember where you came from. God will take care of you. Now, go and see Mary before you lose your nerve. I will be with you in spirit."

As Kris entered room 203 of the hospital trauma unit, he saw a person wrapped up in bandages from just under her nose, all around her head, and down to her neck and shoulders. She was sleeping, or he thought she was. Her eyes were closed, with her bed propped up. Kris wondered if he should say anything or leave.

Mary wasn't asleep. She kept her eyes closed as she raised her hand to motion to whoever entered to place what they had on the bedside table beside her, thinking it was a pitcher of water or her medicine.

When Kris said, "I'm sorry," her eyes popped open and glared in his direction.

Was this the guy who did this to her? Her eyes focused on Kris as she realized who this person was. He was the athlete she had met on the beach in St. Petersburg. Had he hit the foul ball? She was in shock because she had dreamt of seeing him again. The doctors had already told her that her singing career was probably over due to the injury. She was mad at everyone, but especially that ballplayer who hit her. Why did it have to be him? Tears started to trickle down her bandaged cheeks. She couldn't say a word, even though she tried, but the pain was too much.

Seeing the tears swelling in her eyes, Kris got the hint and asked, "Do you need me to leave?" He did not recognize her. "I'm so sorry. Is there anything I can do for you? If I could take it back, I would. Please forgive me." Kris turned and headed out the door as his heart sank in utter despair. All he could think about was what would happen to her. "Will she be okay?" "God, why did you let this happen?"

Chapter 16

HOME

Mary was lying in a hospital bed with bandages still hiding her face. Her thoughts reverted to when she learned of her mother's marriage to Lynn, the local Caledonia High School football coach. She thought about her reaction when her mother informed her about their marriage. What hurt most was that she wasn't there. She had not been invited. The wedding had occurred while she was in North Dakota visiting her cousin, Diane. Her mother didn't include her in any of the plans or events of their marriage. Mary remembered her mother saying she was her best friend. So why would she exclude her best friend from her wedding? Her first major tragedy was losing her father. This was the second major tragedy in Mary's life. This one her mother had created. It was a shocking disappointment and hurt deep down in her soul.

Mary's third tragedy had now happened. She lost her voice. She couldn't talk, much less sing. Singing was her whole life. What is the meaning of living if you can't pursue and enjoy doing what your life's ambition is? The thrill and enjoyment in the experience gained from gigs, traveling to the events, being with your friends, and meeting new people, was gone. It was in the past, and according to the doctors, that joy would never return. The cherished feelings and rewards had vanished. She shouted out loud, "What is the reason for living? What purpose do I have in looking for tomorrow? If tomorrow is not enjoyable and exciting, why do you desire to live past today?" "*Why*" had become the focal part of all her questions. Mary just lay in her hospital bed feeling sorry for herself. Other ideas intermittently entered her mind but lasted only a few moments as she kept reminding herself of her sorrowful situation.

Mary was all alone. Diane had returned to Tennessee to continue her schooling. Walter told Mary he was returning to New York to get her tomorrow and was bringing along a surprise.

"I hope it's not my mother," Mary said as she glanced out the hospital window, seeing nothing but blue sky. That was not true, as she deeply needed her mother. She was still mad at her but secretly desired her to come.

Mary closed her eyes as her thoughts drifted to her Mama Cossitt. Mama always said, "Turn to the Lord in your time of need. Take your problems to the Lord in prayer. He will always answer them in His way." Mary remembered singing the song in church that had those words. She wished Mama were with her now because she would have all the answers to her questions. In Mary's eyes, her Mama was the smartest person she knew and the best friend to turn to in her hour of need. With her eyes closed, she dreamt that Mama was with her now, hugging her, and telling her everything would be okay.

A sudden noise brought Mary back to reality. Her attention turned toward the hospital room door as it was flung open. In the doorway stood Walter with a broad smile, saying, "How is my favorite singer doing?"

Mary looked up and was pleased to see him, though you couldn't tell it from under her bandages. Walter wasn't supposed to be here until tomorrow. No one had told her he was coming early. This was a much-needed surprise.

As Walter entered the hospital room, he said, "I have brought you a wonderful surprise. This woman loves you very much. She is right behind me."

Gale turned the corner and entered the room, saying, "I came to help my little girl." She reached out her arms to Mary, and Mary did the same. They both repeated the words, I love you, as they cried and hugged each other.

Mary drew a sigh of relief. Her mother had not forgotten about her. *She still loves me. I'm still her little girl.*

While they embraced, Walter spoke. "We have come to take you home. Your mother has your room ready and has taken off work. You will receive the special care you need for the next three weeks. I have made all the necessary arrangements. We are packing you up. Home is where you belong."

The doctors had released Mary early as they knew she would be better off in familiar surroundings with people who loved her. The nurses helped gather her things, getting her ready. The pharmacist came to her room to describe her medication, telling her how often to take it and what effects she should experience. He also told her what side effects to watch out for.

Gale was taught how to change the bandages, when to do so, and when she could start leaving them off. Both doctors and nurses emphasized that her voice would not return for at least six months. Then it would be harsh and deep. The prognosis after that was unclear. They could not tell until the swelling went down to see how much damage had been done. Mary needed to return to New York sometime in December before Christmas for further evaluation.

Finally, Mary, Gale, and Walter entered a cab heading for the airport and the ride home to Mississippi. It would be a long six months. Hopefully, as time passed, she would heal both physically and mentally.

Chapter 17

WEDDING PLANNING

It was 30 degrees below zero on a Friday evening in 1969 when Bob received a phone call from Diane. The middle of January in Fargo, with snow blowing and cold temperatures, is not a pretty sight. When it snows one or more inches, it piles up and is dry snow. When the wind blows, like it always does in North Dakota, the snow acts like small needles hitting your face, causing a painful sting. You do not want to be out in the weather very long.

Diane wanted to discuss their wedding plans, which were now only four months away. "We can't talk long because the rates are still pretty high at this time of night. How is my handsome man this evening?"

"Fantastic," Bob replied. "A little cold and dreary, but overall okay. I miss you. I can hardly wait until June. Did you get my letter with the suggestions for people I'd like to invite to our wedding, the best man and groomsmen, and the ushers? Was there anything else I needed to do?"

"I got your letter yesterday. I was going to call you last night, but I also received a letter from Mary telling me about the doctor's scheduled appointment she had on the 28th of December. She found out the damage to her larynx was severe, with little hope of being repaired. The doctor told her there were only two specialists in this country who might be able to fix the problem, and they were expensive. There was also no guarantee that she could be fixed. She said her voice was soft and hoarse sometimes, but understandable, and seemed to be getting better. After reading the entire letter, I called her, planning to talk for only a few minutes. It ended up being three hours. That's why I didn't call you last night. I also told her I would call her back after visiting with you, and we made our final arrangements."

"That's okay, sweetheart," Bob replied. "I hope you can afford that phone call when your bill arrives. What do you think about our guest list and my groomsmen? Can you think of any changes?"

Diane said, "I like your list, but who is your best man? Is it your father or Kris?"

"I've thought long and hard about that question. I would love it if it were Kris, but I decided that my father would be my best man. Kris will be next to my father."

Bob then asked, "How about you? Is your mom the maid of honor, or is it Mary?"

"I'm not sure that Mary will even come to our wedding. She says she doesn't have any money and hasn't worked since the accident. I need to plan on Mom and hope Mary finds a way to attend. I want Mary to play the piano for our wedding. I'm going to ask her when I call her back tomorrow. The problem is that if Mary finds out that Kris will be there, I know she won't come. She is still very upset about what happened to her career and life. If she sees Kris again, it might not be pretty. She knows who Kris is, but Kris doesn't know her. All Kris saw was a bandaged-up lady in the hospital."

"That could be a problem. We sure don't want World War Three to happen during our wedding," Bob replied. "How will we handle the situation if they both end up coming to the wedding?"

"Let's cross that bridge when and if it happens," Diane said. "Hopefully, it all will work out."

"What about all the other arrangements that need to be made? I mean the preacher, the flowers, the rehearsal dinner, and the church. What else have I forgotten to mention?" asked Bob.

Diane announced, "Everything is taken care of, Bob. Don't worry. It's all under control. When we arrive home, everything will be ready for our special day together. My mother guarantees it. We deserve our day."

"That is absolutely why I love you so much and can't wait until we start our lives together," said Bob. "We'll talk soon, and time will go fast. June will be here before we know it. Miss you, my dearest."

"I miss you too, Bob," Diane replied as tears formed and started running down her cheeks. "Keep in touch and see you soon."

Chapter 18

INVITATION

Mary was sitting at the kitchen table with her mother, Gale. Gale said, "You're so down that I'm worried about you. Don't let depression take over. The winners in life are the ones who overcome the obstacles placed in front of them, fight through them, and overcome."

Mary looked at Gale with a painful expression. "I felt great when I could contribute to our family and help you before your wedding. Then, I took care of myself and had a life. Now, I've lost that ability. I'm not able to earn anything and can't live like this. I get so discouraged and feel so worthless and depressed."

Gale sat there with her mouth open, not knowing what to say. She loved her daughter but had no explanation for what to do next. The telephone rang, breaking the silence. Gale answered, saying, "Hello."

Diane recognized Gale's voice and replied, "Hello, Aunt Gale. How are you and Lynn? Great, I hope."

Gale answered, "We are doing great. Lynn's hard at work with the football players in weight training and off-season activities. I'm staying busy with my jobs and trying to help Mary. How about you?"

Diane replied, "Everything is going great. I'm just finishing up some classwork before the final quarter starts. Bob and I are also trying to finalize our wedding plans. That's why I called. May I please talk to Mary?"

Gale said, "Absolutely," and looked at Mary as she was sitting on the couch. "It's for you." She handed her the phone and left the room.

Mary's mood switched instantly when she heard Diane's voice. She was excited to talk to her favorite cousin and hear more about the wedding plans. Small talk about the wedding seemed to last forever.

Diane finally mustered enough courage to ask Mary how she was doing physically. She wanted to know more about her mental state, but didn't know how to ask. Her voice sounded better each time they talked. Eventually, Diane got around to what she wanted to ask. Diane said, "Mary, will you consider attending our wedding ceremony in North Dakota and playing the piano? Bob and I have some special music we want you to perform."

Mary's reply was instant, "No." Mary's answer to every subsequent request from Diane was an automatic "no."

Diane became flustered with Mary and didn't know what to do or say. Nothing was working, so she decided to hang up before she said something she would regret later.

Mary heard the phone click as she stood up from the couch and walked over to the kitchen table, saying, "Hello, hello. Diane, are you still there?" A humming sound was on the receiver. Mary couldn't believe that Diane had hung up on her.

Diane was upset by the continuous word "no." She needed Mary to be at the wedding. She needed Mary to play a complicated piece of music that only a musician could perform. After thinking about what to do next, she decided on one possible solution. Diane knew only one lady who could change Mary's mind. She picked up the phone and dialed Mama Cossitt.

Mama Cossitt answered on the third ring, "Hello," she said in a sweet tone that reflected her demeanor.

"Mama Cossitt, this is Diane from North Dakota. I need your help. I have asked Mary to play the piano at my wedding. She says the word no every time I ask. She needs to get out of the mood she's in. I worry about her. What can I do to change her mind?"

Mama Cossitt laughed as she gave a frank response. "For her, you need to be firm and not let her say no. Tell her she's going. You expect her to be there with no excuses. Remember, you are in charge, and she will do what you want, no exceptions."

Diane said," Thank you, Mama. I knew you would know what I should do."

Diane redialed Mary's number. When Mary answered, Diane apologized for hanging up the phone on her. Not stopping to let Mary answer, she said, "I won't accept 'no' for an answer. You owe me. I played the piano for you when you needed me in New York at the Sullivan show. Now, you will play the piano at my wedding. I'm mailing you the music so you can practice and be ready to make my wedding special. We are sending you a round-trip plane ticket so you have no excuses. This decision is final, you have no choice. Bob and I will be talking to you later, so get prepared. Make your plans because you're attending our wedding. Goodbye, and thank you."

Mary stood there with her mouth open. The humming sound returned to the telephone. She chuckled at the situation. She realized that Diane needed her as much as she needed Diane. She thought, *maybe this is the ticket for me to get out of the mood I've been in. I need to get my life on track again. Mama Cossitt always said that someone is always looking out for you. All you must do is trust and obey.*

Chapter 19

MEETING AND WEDDING

Diane was thrilled with how the wedding planning had turned out. It's early February, and she and Bob have done a wonderful job coordinating everything for their wedding in June. Luckily, Kris's ball club had decided it was in their best interest to let Kris off for one game during the four-game set from June 3rd through the 6th. The Minnesota Twins were scheduled to play in Los Angeles. Kris would play the first three games. He would leave right after the afternoon third game on the 5th, and fly to North Dakota in time to attend his two best friends' rehearsal dinner and wedding on June 6th. It was a struggle, but the management finally gave their approval. This was the last hurdle for Bob and Diane to get over.

Bob called Diane with the news that Kris had been given the time off, but had to forfeit his earnings for the one game. "No big deal," Kris had said. "I promised them I would not accept payment and would donate an equal amount to the ball club's favorite charity, the Boys and

Girls Club of Northern Minneapolis." This pleased the owner, so it was a done deal.

After talking to Mama Cossitt about Diane's demands, Mary finally decided to attend and realized how important it was to them.

Diane and Bob had everybody and everything ready for their big day. They could now concentrate on their graduation before returning home. Both decided they would attend the other's graduation as they were a week apart. That night in February, Diane told Bob, "Goodnight, sweetheart. In four months, we will be husband and wife. I love you."

Bob's reply was, "I love you, too. Goodnight."

* * * * * * * * * * * * * * * *

Bob picked Kris up at the airport four months later as he flew into Bismarck after his day game in Los Angeles. "How is the season going, Kris? Are you doing okay? I mean, your batting average and fielding?"

Kris responded, "Slow down, buddy. I think you might be getting nervous. Am I right?"

"Some. Maybe a little bit," Bob stuttered. "That's why I need you. Keep me straight for the next two days. Please."

"I'll do my best. It might be a hard job since you are acting like this now. Calm down, and everything will be okay." Kris continued, "Do we need to pick up my tux, or have you decided to wear jeans? Just kidding, Bob. Just trying to lighten up the conversation."

Bob said, "I have picked up your tux and everything is set for this evening's rehearsal dinner. Both Diane and I need you to be ready for the unexpected. Just go with the flow and hopefully, everything will be okay."

"What do you mean?" Kris asked.

"Buddy, just be yourself. It will be fine." Bob said unconvincingly.

"Okay, but let me know if I need to do something," Kris replied.

* * * * * * * * * * * * * * *

Everyone was entering the room for the rehearsal dinner at Ned Bear Paws restaurant when Kris spotted her; the young lady he had met on the beach in Florida was in the room. How could that be? Where had she come from, and who was she? Kris took his seat next to Bob's father, with Diane seated beside Bob. Bob was too far from him to ask questions, and the lady had not noticed him yet. He wanted to get up, go to her, and ask her why she was there, but decided he better not.

Something warned him to be patient. He would talk to her after dinner was over and the formalities completed.

Kris stared straight at her as Mary looked around the room. Her glance passed over him at first, but suddenly turned back toward him with an icy glare and a shocked expression. Kris saw her lean toward Diane, whisper something, and look upset. What was going on? He felt a sudden urge to flee. Is this what Bob had warned him about?

Diane seemed to calm her down. She was as beautiful as he remembered from the beach. He needed to know her name, but she acted like she wanted nothing to do with him. *I need to find out what's going on*, Kris thought. *Maybe after the rehearsal dinner and the actual rehearsal practice, I'll get answers to my questions. She is so beautiful.*

The young lady avoided Kris after dinner and throughout the rehearsal. Kris wanted to ask Diane or Bob about her, but they seemed to go out of their way to avoid him. Suddenly, the light went on. He knew who she was and why Bob had told him to be himself. This had to be Mary. She was the one at the beach he fell head over heels for, and the person in the hospital. She had been hit with the baseball, and the patient was all bandaged up. That had happened accidentally, but he was the cause. Her career had been ruined. The responsibility had fallen on his shoulders. No wonder he received those icy stares.

Diane saw Kris's face change from curiosity to realization as he dropped his head into his hands.

Kris left the auditorium, entered the vestibule, and slumped into a cushioned-back chair.

Diane was close behind him as she excused herself from the rest of the rehearsal party. "I see that you figured out what was happening here tonight. Are you going to be okay, Kris? She doesn't want to talk to you or even be around you. She is still hurting, can't sing, and is trying to find her way. She went from a person on top of the world to rock bottom in twenty-four hours. She told me about the meeting on the beach in Florida, but she can't get over what has happened since. Please be patient with her and give her the space she needs.

"Diane, I'm so sorry for everything. I don't know how the baseball got through the netting. It was a freak accident. If I could take it back, I would," exclaimed Kris. "She is so beautiful. I want to be with her. I want to get to know her."

"Unfortunately, that's not possible now. Give it time. Slow down and give her a chance to get over this," Diane responded.

Kris said, "I will leave as soon as the wedding is over tomorrow. Once I get my hug from you and Bob, I'll head to Los Angeles to join my team. Tell Mary again I'm so sorry for everything, and I hope she can forgive me."

The wedding the next day went on without a hitch. Diane was beautiful in her white gown with lace trim. The men's blue tuxes with yellow roses complemented the ladies' light-yellow dresses with blue and white corsages, making it a wonderful event. The first bridesmaid, Bob's sister Barb, proceeded down the aisle, followed by Margaret, Diane's mother, and the maid of honor. Smiles on their faces resembled the bright sun in all its glory. The ring bearer, Ezra, followed them as he pranced down the aisle, showing off his soccer-style movements. The audience marveled at his enthusiasm. Everly and Elliott came next, spreading red rose petals as they processed. It was now Diane's moment to shine, as her father escorted her toward the front of the church. Her beautiful white-laced wedding gown was a sight to behold. Every inch of her exclaimed the love she was showing for Bob.

Diane and Bob held hands during the entire service. They each proclaimed their vows and placed their rings on their left finger. During the vows, Diane started to tear up and could hardly talk. Bob squeezed her hand just a smidge to help her through her words, which was all she needed. His assurance was calming. The preacher announced that you may now kiss the bride. The kiss was passionate and beautiful. They turned toward the crowd, and the preacher announced, "May I present Mr. and Mrs. Bob Johnson.

Mary had played the piano perfectly. Kris and the other groomsman, Bob's father, could see tears in her eyes as the wedding concluded.

Kris was true to his word. After the wedding, he hugged Diane and Bob, shook Bob's hand, wished them well, and headed toward the airport. He had to get his mind back on baseball and forget about Mary. He was having a fantastic season, hitting .359, with 18 homers by June, and knocking in 47 runs. Kris was on pace to garner a most-valuable player award by year's end.

Mary saw him leave. Purposely, they had not talked over the time of the celebration. Diane gave Mary Kris's message. Her emotions were torn in several directions, but she couldn't forgive him. He had two strikes against him: running over her on the beach and hitting a foul ball that struck her and changed her life.

Chapter 20

HOME AGAIN

This was the best Mary had felt in a long time. It was Sunday morning, the day after the wedding. She was sitting in the pew of the Riverwood Independent Church in Riverwood, North Dakota. During the reception, she had promised Pastor Ron that she would attend the morning service at his invitation. Everyone had enjoyed Diane's and Bob's wedding the night before. Mary had played the piano as they had wished, but deep down inside, she had hoped to sing a song for the occasion. Though singing wasn't possible, she felt good about herself and knew somehow, she would be alright.

As she sat reading the morning bulletin, Pastor Michael and his wife, Ashley, approached the pew. Michael asked, "May we sit with you? Are you all alone, or is someone coming to be with you this morning?"

"No, I'm by myself," Mary replied. "Please join me. I feel a little lonesome." She was excited about seeing them and wanted them to sit with her.

Pastor Michael was Bob's good friend and classmate in seminary school. He helped Pastor Ron perform the wedding. Both pastors did an excellent job. Their deep and loud voices made it easy for all the wedding attendees to hear each word as they performed their duties.

Pastor Ron was also a friend of Diane and Bob. He graduated from the same seminary school as Bob and Michael, but two years before them. He was now the regular pastor at the church and would speak at the Sunday worship service. All three pastors, Bob, Michael, and Ron, were exciting to be around as they constantly discussed topics about the Bible. Sometimes, they would even argue, but always remained friends.

Mary's bulletin read the name of the upcoming sermon, "*Vagabond and Wanderer, what does the Bible say?*" *I have no idea what that's about. It seems strange,* she thought. *I hope I can understand what he is talking about. I might need to have Michael explain it to me later.*

The organ music began, indicating the beginning of the service. Mary's attention was diverted to the aisle as a lady approached and sat beside Pastor Michael. She was the wife of Pastor Ron. Mary thought how fortunate Diane and Bob were to have such great friends. She realized she had no one her age. She didn't even have a boyfriend. The message was a blur as she was thinking more about her life situation than concentrating on what the pastor said. Mary missed the whole service but heard the final question.

Pastor Ron closed the church service by asking the congregation, "What are you in your world? Are you a Vagabond, a Wanderer, or are you settled, fixed, and rooted in your faith?" After a few more announcements, the organist began playing, indicating the service was ending.

Michael had promised Bob that he and Ashley would take Mary to the Campsite Grill for a good meal before returning to Bismarck and catching an airplane back to Mississippi. This was Diane and Bob's favorite restaurant. They each enjoyed a delicious ribeye steak with all the added sides that came along with it. There were wonderful-tasting green beans, mashed potatoes with scrumptious white gravy, and a salad mixed with lettuce, carrots, cheese, eggs, cucumbers, bacon bits, and croutons. The meal was topped off with a delicious red velvet cake. They were all full and happily satisfied. Ashley and Michael accompanied Mary to the airport and stayed with her until she boarded the plane for her flight home.

Mary had a lot of time to think about her situation on the airplane. When she had her voice and was performing, she felt like somebody special. People loved her. They wanted her autograph. Now, everything had changed. Was it Kris's fault she couldn't sing? He hadn't hit her with the ball on purpose. It was a freak accident. Why was she blaming him? Mary's thoughts drifted toward the Bible. Mama Cossitt always said it was the book with all the answers to your questions. God will always take care of you no matter what situation arises. As she drifted into a relaxed sleep, she thought, *Why has God not taken care of me?*

Chapter 21

Baseball and Pain

Kris's return to the majors after the wedding was a momentous occasion. In his first at-bat, he hit a monstrous homer straight over the centerfield wall that almost left the ballpark. It measured 489 feet, and the speed of the ball off the bat was an amazing 110 miles per hour. He threw all his energy into baseball. He couldn't think about the past any longer. He had to forget about the young lady on the beach named Mary because she had ignored him during their appearance at the wedding. He was not able to handle the rejection any longer.

All aspects of his game clicked at the same time. It was only June, he had three more months of baseball before the playoffs started. He made the most of that time. Kris impressed the coaches and front office with his playmaking in the infield during games.

On one occasion during a game in Boston, the Red Sox had a runner on third base with only one out. The batter hit a soft fly ball toward right-center field. The outfielders were playing too deep to get to the ball. Kris sprinted full speed toward the outfield with his back to home plate. He knew if he caught the ball, it would be difficult to stop, gain his footing, turn, and fire the ball to home plate to get the runner tagging up at third base heading for home. As the right fielder was heading in his direction, Kris stretched out as far as he could reach and caught the ball in the webbing of his glove. As he was stumbling after the catch, he saw the right fielder coming toward him. He grabbed the ball with his right hand and flipped it to the right fielder with a cannon for an arm. The right fielder caught the ball with his bare hand and launched the ball toward home plate. The catcher caught the ball, tagging out the runner by at least three feet. Boston failed to score any runs that day.

In Minnesota, two days later, an opposing batter hit a foul ball behind first base down the line toward the bleachers. The bases were loaded with two outs, and Kris's team, the Twins, were ahead by one run in the bottom of the ninth inning. Kris was playing second base when he, the first baseman, and the right fielder converged on the ball. Nobody knew if they could get there in time to catch the ball. Neither of the fielders called the other off as they headed to the point of contact. Kris dove with his glove outstretched as the right fielder and first baseman collided, bouncing off each other on their way to the ground. Kris felt the ball hit his glove as he slid into the wall. Everyone was okay, and it was the third out, ending the game. That play made every highlight film on all the sports channels for the next two days.

Kris didn't make any errors for the rest of the season. He won the Rawlings Golden Glove Award as the best second baseman in the league. This award was special and coveted by all baseball players.

Kris also won the highest batting average in the league. He had the most hits. The most doubles and triples of any player. This made him one of the favorites to win the Most Valuable Player Award at the season's end.

The front office and the owner of the ball team feared losing Kris at year's end because his contract was up for renewal. They offered him a one-million-dollar contract with a signing bonus of another five hundred thousand if he signed a new contract before the end of the season. He loved it in Minnesota, so his agent ensured him it was guaranteed money with no stipulations before signing the dotted line. Even if he got hurt, the money was his.

While at the Fill & Chill restaurant and bar one evening on his day off, he ran into a former acquaintance he had met during his wild days in college. She was a beautiful blonde lady. Being five feet eight inches tall, she was admired by every young man in the establishment. Her skin-tight outfit proclaimed her healthiness and desire.

Cindy approached Kris, saying, "Aren't you the baseball player from college that I met at a party in Fargo a few years back?"

"Why yes, it's good to see you again," replied Kris with a smile. "You're in Minnesota now. What brought you here?"

"After I graduated from business school, I got a job with a law firm on Fifth Avenue in the city." Cindy continued, "You have been doing fantastically with the Twins. I have kept up with your statistics since I'm a baseball fan. You remember that from our days in Fargo, don't you?"

"Sure do," Kris exclaimed. "Some of the parties we went to were pretty wild, if I remember. Some are still a blur."

They continued talking and were attracted to each other. One thing led to another, and this beautiful blonde invited him to her apartment for what she called a nightcap. Kris wasn't sure about this but decided, what the heck, why not? He had no one to answer to.

After entering the apartment, Cindy made her move on him. As she started kissing him on the neck and unbuttoning his shirt, he closed his eyes. He was enjoying this immensely. The shirt was fully unbuttoned and was being pulled out of his pants. Suddenly, he opened his eyes. Right in front of him was a full-length mirror. What he saw in the mirror shook him to the core. There was a picture of a man and a woman walking in the sand on a beach.

Kris shouted, "Stop, I can't do this. I have already given my heart away. There's a special brunette that I can't get out of my mind." He put his hands on Cindy's shoulders, nudging her away. Quickly, he buttoned his shirt, grabbed his things, and headed for the door. "I'm sorry," he said as he shut the door, heading for the safety of his home. Right then, he knew he would not give up trying to win over the love of his life.

Everything went great for the rest of the season. The Twins won all their playoff games, making it to the World Series, the summit of professional baseball. In game one of the seven-game series, Kris hit a booming homer, driving in three runs as Minnesota won by a score of 3 to 1. He was not so fortunate during the second game. Kris had singled to center and was on first base when the next batter drove a ball into deep short, headed for left field. The opposing team's shortstop dove for the ball, catching it on a miraculous play. He had no play at first, so he threw the ball toward second base. Kris was hustling, trying to get there before the ball. During his slide, the spike on his left foot caught in the dirt, creating a wrenching pain in his left ankle. He was safe, but his ankle was not. He had to be carried off the field into a waiting ambulance headed for the hospital. Minnesota won the World Series despite Kris being hurt. Kris's season was over, and surgery was upcoming.

Chapter 22

BAD NEWS

After Mary returned to Mississippi from Diane and Bob's wedding, she felt emotionally stable for a few days. She was upbeat and seemed to be back to her cheerful and pleasant self. Her smile was addictive. She helped Gale around the house, cleaning and cooking meals. She was on it immediately if something needed to be done, like the dishes or grocery shopping. She didn't need to be asked. That continued until a letter arrived from her physician, Doctor Tim, in New York.

Mary's mother, Gale, told her husband, Lynn, "When Mary opened the letter, she was so excited because she expected to hear good news. As she started reading, I could see from the reaction in her eyes that something was wrong. I saw a concerned look that quickly changed to tears. She tore the paper to shreds, crumpled it up, and threw it into the burn pile that had been lit. Mary ran to her room and slammed the door shut. I've tried to talk to her, but she won't say anything about the letter or what it said. Now, she mopes around and acts like there's nothing worth living for. Lynn, will you please try talking to her? I've tried, but have gotten nowhere."

Lynn said, "Let's give her a couple of days first, and see how she responds to us. If that doesn't work by this weekend, I'll see what I can do."

By Saturday morning, Mary hadn't talked or communicated with anyone. Lynn approached her bedroom door, banged loudly, and said, "Get ready. We're going to breakfast in ten minutes, and to say no is not an option. I'll be waiting at the front door."

She knew it was useless to resist. She had come to admire him and considered him more and more to be the father she never had due to the war. The more Mary had been around him, the closer they had become. She trusted him because he was honest, true, and sincere. He was the closest person she ever considered discussing her problems with, except for Mama Cossitt. Mary dressed hurriedly, brushed her hair, and met Lynn on his way out the door, headed for the car. "Where are we going to eat?" asked Mary.

"I'm treating you at my favorite place, the Caledonia Ember and Elm restaurant. You know that's the only place I go. I met your mother there when she was the top waitress. She always made me feel special with her super service." Lynn continued, "I'll not go anywhere else."

After eating and drinking their second cup of coffee, Lynn said, "Okay, it's time to talk. I'm not only a football coach to my young players, Mary, but also a leader, a doctor, a counselor, and sometimes a pastor. I try my best to help each of them. I can't show partiality or favoritism. I need to be there when they need me. They have to trust me, and you have to do the same. Now, what's wrong? What did the letter say?"

Mary hesitated for only a second. "The letter said that I would not get any better without surgery, an expensive surgery. Time won't work. It's more money than I could ever imagine. It's hopeless."

"Mary, God may have taken away one of your talents, but you have many more. Don't be defeated by losing one. Use your others to become a better person and a winner. I have three rules in life. They work, and I want to share them with you. Don't ever forget them. First, you are standing on train tracks in front of the train. You can decide whether to get run over, get out of the way, or get on the train of life and go forward at full speed. Second, there are three types of people in the world: those who make things happen, those who watch things happen, and those who wonder what happened. I say, make something happen. Third, the scenery will never change unless you are the lead dog pulling the sled. Be a leader in life and make it happen. Your mother and I will support you all the way."

Mary thought about what Lynn had said for the rest of the day. "He's right," she said. "I need to get on with my life. Go forward and not look back."

That evening, Mary called Diane. When Diane answered, Mary said, "Is there some work I can do in the church? Can I play the piano or teach music? I want to come to North Dakota and learn more about the Bible from you and Bob. Is this possible?"

Diane screamed, "Yes, I'll be at the airport when your plane arrives. Please send me the details. You are welcome to stay as long as you need to. You have made me very happy. God bless you. See you soon."

Mary replied, "I'll be in touch. Thank you. Bye."

Chapter 23

SURGERY

Kris's surgery for his broken ankle lasted for three hours. The ankle was fractured in two places. Small rods had to be strategically placed to ensure proper healing with the least damage to mobility in the future. He feared that his career might be over because the damage had been so severe, but the doctors assured him that was not going to happen. He would return as good as new after several months of healing and rehabbing.

Lying in bed in the Minnesota hospital was no fun at all. His foot was elevated with a sling to prevent blood clots and reduce swelling. His days were filled with uninteresting television and distasteful meals. Every time he tried to sleep, he would be awakened by staff checking on him or nurses wanting to check his vital signs. The worst part of the experience was using a bedpan and urinal when it was time to go to the bathroom. Both were embarrassing and difficult to accomplish.

A few of his teammates came by after they won the World Series to celebrate. Kris enjoyed seeing them and had a great time rehashing the games, but something was missing. When they left, he was all alone. That's what bothered him the most.

Each day dragged by as Kris lay there. He tried reading books and magazines and even had a movie projector brought in to view the latest releases. It had only been five days, but nothing seemed to satisfy him as his anxiety grew to the point of depression. He didn't know what to do, so he asked his old friends for help.

Kris called Diane from his hospital bed. "Hello," Kris managed to say as she answered the phone. "How are you and Bob today?"

"Better than you are, I'm sure, Kris." Diane said, "We heard about your accident. It's been all over the sports reports every night as the announcers rehashed the games and then talked about your injury. I'm glad your team won the World Series, but I am sorry you couldn't be there to celebrate with them. How are you feeling? Were the doctors able to fix your ankle?"

"I think they did a good job, at least that's what I've been told. I'll have a cast put on tomorrow, and then it's time to learn to walk with crutches. I'm not looking forward to that at all," replied Kris. "Hopefully, I won't fall too many times."

"You sound very depressed, Kris. Are you sure you're okay? Have you had much company?" asked Diane.

"No." That's all Diane heard when Kris finally answered her. Then he said, "My parents have been busy harvesting the corn, so they aren't able to leave the farm right now."

"Well, I've got some good news for you." Diane continued, "I wasn't going to tell you, but you need encouragement. You should see a familiar face in a couple of hours. Bob left here this morning after breakfast and headed for Minnesota. The last time I talked to him, he was about three hours away. That was an hour ago. We both thought some cheering up from lifelong friends might help."

"Thank you, Diane. I needed to hear your voice. Now I get to see Bob. This day can't get any better. Both of you are what I was wishing for. Thanks," said Kris.

Diane continued, "Now don't tell Bob I told you and give away his surprise. Get some rest, and he should be there soon. Love you. Get well soon."

"I love you also. Thanks for being there for me," Kris said as he hung up the phone and drifted off to sleep. Soon, his best friend would be there.

* * * * * * * * * * * * * * *

Two hours later, there was a tapping on Kris's hospital room door. He had fallen into a deep, restful sleep after talking to Diane. It had relaxed him so much that this was his best sleep in the last three days. As he tried to wake himself from the deep state, he said, "Come in." He had forgotten that Bob was on his way.

"Hello, buddy. How are you doing? I hope I didn't wake you."

"It's okay. Bob, what a surprise. It's great to see a friendly face instead of the doctors and nurses all the time. How are you, and how is Diane?"

"We're great, but have been worried about you. We watched the accident on television. You were carried off on a stretcher!" Bob continued, "Diane and I have been worried sick since then, so I decided to take two days off and come to Minnesota. I see your ankle in the sling. What's next?"

Kris replied, "Tomorrow I get a cast put on and fitted for crutches. They told me I had to keep my leg elevated with little movement for I forgot how long, and then eventually I'll be able to move around on the crutches until the ankle heals. That's when the cast comes off and the rehab starts. They couldn't tell how long that would take. They said it depends on me. How much I put into it, and how much pain I can stand. I don't know because I've never been through this before."

Bob asked, "Are you going to stay in your apartment in Minneapolis, or somewhere else? You'll need help getting around and someone to wait on you until you're more comfortable on those crutches."

"My agent is taking care of that, so don't worry. I'll be fine," said Kris. "Let's talk about you and Diane. How's married life?"

"Everything is great. We've gotten settled in our new house and jobs. Diane is working at the school, and I'm working as the assistant pastor at the church. Sometimes she works at the church too. We both enjoy what we're doing. Saturday is our day, just being together.

They continued talking for the rest of the evening until Bob saw Kris try to hide a slight yawn, and he knew it was time to leave. The nurses had just been in to check Kris's blood pressure and other vital signs. Bob got up from the chair he was sitting in, indicating to Kris that it was time to leave.

Kris asked, "Do you think that if I come to Bismarck to do my rehab, that would cause any problem?"

"Of course not," replied Bob. "Why would you ask such a crazy question? We'd love to be able to see you more."

"The Twins baseball club has a farm team in Bismarck, and their best rehab center is located at Med Center One Hospital," Kris said. "I've researched it and will probably come there for my rehab session. When that's over, I hope to be ready for spring training when it begins."

"Just let us know. We'd be glad to spend more time with you," Bob replied. "Diane sends her love. See you later, brother. It's great to see and visit with you again, even under these circumstances. We've missed you."

"Thanks for coming, Bob. You know I love you both. Be careful driving home," Kris answered. "I'll not say bye, but just see you later."

With that, Bob was gone, and Kris was alone in his thoughts again. It was wonderful to see Bob, and his spirits had been raised tremendously.

Chapter 24

REHAB AND DATE?

Four months after Kris left the hospital in Minneapolis on crutches, he arrived in Bismarck to start his rehab training. He had around a month and a half before spring training, so he hoped that would be enough time to prepare him to rejoin the Twins in Florida. The first few days were brutal. The cast had recently been removed, but he still wanted to use the crutches, since the ankle was still sore with the additional weight. Gradually, as the days went by, he regained motion and strength in the ankle as the therapists did their magic. The encouraging results made Kris's demeanor more positive. He could envision himself back on the diamond playing the game he loved.

During rehab, Diane, Bob, and his parents had visited him in Bismarck several times. They had asked him to come to Riverwood for a visit, but it had never worked out. The team required rehab training every day of the week to make sure he would be ready for spring training. Besides that, he did not want to return home except to see Diane and Bob. His dad wanted him to quit baseball and work with him on the farm. That was not an option, so why go home? He could have worked it out if he truly wanted, but there was no reason. He didn't know Mary was only an hour away, working at the church. Kris missed her, but his pride always got in the way of asking Diane about her.

One Wednesday afternoon, Mary had just finished the piano lessons with her tenth student of the day. As she walked by Diane's office door, she could see that Diane wasn't busy. She entered saying, "How are you today?"

Diane replied, "Not so bad. The bulletin is done for Sunday, and the monthly newsletter is completed. It's ready to mail out tomorrow. How about you? Are you ready for choir practice tonight? They enjoy the way you play that baby grand."

"I've practiced the hymns several times," Mary said. "I sure wish I could sing with you. Anyway, that's not the reason I stopped by. Out of curiosity, have you heard anything from your friend during the off-season? I mean, is he okay after his injury? I was just wondering."

Diane was taken by surprise. Had she forgiven him? Did she like him, or was she just being nice? She had never told Mary that he was in Bismarck doing rehab on his ankle, and that's who they went to see on their trips when she wasn't invited to go along. "He's rehabbing his ankle, and it's about to be one hundred percent ready for spring training. Why do you ask?"

"Just curious," Mary said. "Glad he is doing okay. Well, I'd better run. See you at choir."

With that, she was gone. Mary left the choir as soon as it was over, so Diane had no opportunity to ask her about their earlier conversation. She had gotten an apartment by then and had become very independent. That didn't stop Diane from talking with Bob about Mary's questions later that evening.

Bob said, "Maybe we should try again to get them together. Kris seems so lonely at times. It could be that Mary has forgiven him, or that she is lonely, too. What do you think?"

"I think it's worth a try. Kris will be done with rehab next week, so let's set something up for this weekend."

Diane and Bob had to persuade Mary and Kris to agree to a blind date on Saturday evening. Neither knew who was coming, and they didn't like dates with people they didn't know. Both trusted Diane and Bob, so ultimately, they agreed since all four would be on a double date.

Kris saw Mary first as he entered the restaurant. He was shocked, but his thoughts returned to the beautiful woman he had met on the beach. *What are Diane and Bob up to?*

When Mary realized who her blind date was, she was stunned. She was the first to talk. "What are you doing here?"

Diane stopped Kris before he could speak. She said in a stern voice, "You two need to talk! Get over your stubbornness. Both of you are lonely and need a friend. Bob and I will be at another table until you get this hashed out. No shouting, and remember that God loves you both."

Kris talked first. "I'm sorry you got hurt. Your career was starting to bloom, and your voice was truly a blessing. I regret that I ruined everything. If I could reverse everything that happened, I'd do it in a heartbeat."

Mary said, "I know it wasn't your fault. I should have been paying attention to what was happening instead of signing autographs and accepting congratulations. You don't need to blame yourself. I can't get over a ball striking me. It's a nightmare that happens over and over."

"Is there anything I can do to stop the nightmares?" Kris asked.

"No," Mary replied. "It's something I have to get over myself. Nobody can help me. Maybe time will take care of it."

Surprisingly, they talked for another thirty minutes. Mary said, "I have been working in North Dakota for the past few months, teaching piano lessons and playing piano for the church. Winter has shown so much beauty when the snowflakes fall. Events like the snow and ice don't happen in the South, where I live. The wind is a negative in my eyes. On cold days, it cuts right through you like a knife slicing butter, which makes me shiver and shake."

Kris spoke up next. "I've been bored in the hospital for the last month and a half. I wish I had known you were in Riverwood all this time. I would have called you sooner, hoping to be your friend. We all need someone to talk to. Hopping around on crutches and not getting around or going places has made me depressed. Having someone check on me daily to make sure I behave myself has not been pleasant. It's not what I desire in life. I like to choose who I see and not be told."

Mary replied, "You sound upset. I know what being depressed feels like; I've been there. Yet, you'll be able to return to baseball in a few weeks, that should make you happy."

"It does," said Kris. "I'm sorry. I have been talking about myself and not listening to you, especially your voice. Are you going to be able to sing anytime soon?

Mary looked down at the floor. "The doctor said I would never sing again unless I have surgery that costs more money than I could ever dream of. There's no hope, so I'm trying to get on with my life and use my other talents to help people.

After Mary said that, neither knew what to say next, and both struggled to find words, so they finally turned to look at Diane and Bob.

Diane and Bob realized they had stopped talking, but everything looked okay. They rejoined them then for a nice evening. After eating, they went to a show, walked through the mall together window shopping, ate ice cream, and had a pleasant conversation about anything you could imagine.

Kris asked Mary, "Tell me about the children you are teaching. How old are they?"

Mary said, "They range from age six to twelve. They are so sweet and try so hard to please me."

"How about your band back home?" Kris asked. "Are they still playing together, and have you ever considered playing the piano for them?"

"Sure, I have," replied Mary. "It's just so hard to do and not be able to sing like I used to."

Mary, in turn, asked Kris about baseball and what little she knew about it. "Do you have fun playing a game all the time? Playing baseball would become boring to me, doing the same thing every day."

Kris laughed. "I can see why you might think that. It's a sport that I live for and enjoy.

"How about the farm? Have you ever considered returning home to help your family?" she asked.

"No," is all he said. It did make him think about it, though, as he couldn't play baseball forever.

The time to leave and head home came too soon, as everyone had a good time.

Before they parted, Kris got Diane off to the side and asked two questions. "Who was Mary's doctor, and was there anything that could be done to help her get her voice back?"

Diane told him to talk to Gale. Quickly, she wrote down her name and phone number as they headed for the car.

Kris looked at Diane, Bob, and Mary and said, "I had a wonderful evening. Mary, thank you for talking to me. I hope someday your nightmares go away, and you'll be able to enjoy life to the fullest again."

Mary smiled at Kris and waved goodbye, and an enjoyable evening ended in a pleasant parting.

The next morning, Kris called Gale. After introducing himself, he asked, "I understand that Mary's surgery to regain her voice is expensive. Can you arrange it with the doctor without Mary knowing where the money came from? Can you say it came from a foundation or something? I want to help her."

Gale replied, "Are you the person who hit the baseball?"

"Yes," he said. "This is something that I feel I need to do for her. She deserves a chance to sing. Most of all, I want her to be happy."

Gale said, "If you are sure, I will call Doctor Tim in New York. He would have to make all the arrangements."

"Thank you. And please, Mary must not know," reiterated Kris. "I'll send the money immediately, just let me know where." With that, he gave Gale his address and phone number.

"If that is your wish," Gale said with a questioning voice. "I will see to it right away. Thank you, and someday I hope to thank you in person."

* * * * * * * * * * * * * * * *

Seven days later, Mary received a call from her doctor. Mary was teaching a piano lesson when the church secretary interrupted her, saying, "You have a call in the office from Doctor Tim. He said it was important."

"Can he call me back in twenty minutes when the child's lesson is over?" Mary asked.

"The doctor sounded like it was urgent. I think you should take it," replied the secretary.

Mary hurried to the office and said, "Okay, go ahead. I'm listening."

"Mary, I am sending you a letter," he began. "This letter contains the name of a doctor, Doctor Paul. I recommended him, and he agreed to do your surgery. He practices in Birmingham, Alabama, and works with the Birmingham Voice Foundation. He is the best in his field. He has agreed to take your case and will accept what the foundation has offered for payment. You should be able to sing again!"

Mary was speechless. She didn't know what to say. Mary heard a small voice coming from her mouth saying, "Thank you," as she hung up the phone. Not knowing what to say or do, she just stood there in shock.

She returned to the class where her child waited patiently, wondering what to do next.

The student asked, "Is my lesson over?"

Mary answered, "Just practice for the next fifteen minutes, then you can leave. Have a nice afternoon."

Mary headed directly to Diane's office and tapped on the door.

Diane opened the door and said, "Mary, you are white as a sheet! Are you okay?"

Mary exclaimed, "I'm going to sing again!"

"What do you mean?" Diane answered.

"I just got a call from my doctor in New York. A Doctor in Birmingham has taken my case and agreed to do the surgery. A foundation is paying for it," Mary said as she tried to think.

"That's fantastic," said Diane. "How soon and when?"

"I don't know until I get the letter. The letter will go to my address in Mississippi. Diane, I need to go home."

* * * * * * * * * * * * * * * *

Three days later, on Saturday morning, Mary was sitting on her front porch waiting for the mail to arrive. Maybe this was the day she would get the letter. The postman came by the mailbox, and as she watched, he put several letters in the box. She hurriedly jumped off the porch and headed to see if it was there. Sure enough, a letter arrived from New York with Doctor Tim's address on it. As she ripped it open, the other letters went flying. "I'll pick them up later," she said out loud as she started to read.

Mary's appointment with Doctor Paul was next Monday at 9:00 a.m. Dr. Tim had sent all her records to him. The blood work, multiple X-rays, and ultrasounds were all in his packet. Any other tests he needed could be done in his office. She was so encouraged that she ran into the house, hugging her mom and Lynn before calling Diane. Next Monday was the day she'd been praying for, and she couldn't wait for it to come.

Meanwhile, Kris was in Florida at spring training. His hitting and fielding were as slick as before the injury. He picked up right where he left off, expecting a great season to come.

Mary and Kris each seemed to have a new lease on life, but would that continue? The big question is: are they going to be happy?

Chapter 25

DOCTOR PAUL

It was a bright, sunny Monday morning for Mary and Gale. They left home in Caledonia, Mississippi, and drove to UAB Hospital in Birmingham, Alabama. Lynn didn't go along due to his commitments at Caledonia High School. Gale promised him she would call immediately after Mary's medical evaluation.

After arrival, they parked in the closest lot next to the building at the address given in the instructions. Mary and Gale entered the professional building by the hospital, looking for Doctor Paul Kirk's office. The nurse informed Gale that the evaluation was the first step in treating Mary. Also, an overnight stay may be required to conduct all the necessary tests.

Mary and Gale located the doctor's office with help from the employees at the information desk. As they entered, Mary went to the sign-in desk, wrote her name down, and the receptionist said, "Please have a seat. We'll be with you shortly." It wasn't two minutes later when the receptionist called, "Mary, please come to the front desk." She handed Mary a stack of papers. "Please fill out this questionnaire and sign the treatment forms. You need not bother with the insurance forms; that part has been completed. There is also a page about your medical history. When you are finished filling them out, please return them to me so I can enter them in your chart. It shouldn't be long after that when Doctor Paul will be ready to see you."

After finishing the paperwork, Mary and Gale sat in the lobby patiently waiting for Mary's name to be called. They both were saying silent prayers for a great visit and a positive outcome.

Doctor Tim, in New York, had informed Mary that he believed she had a fractured larynx but didn't know how severe it was. He thought she would never sing again, but he wasn't a specialist in that field of medicine. He had heard of Doctor Kirk, who was a specialist. If anyone could help her, he was the one who could by giving a specific diagnosis of Mary's true condition.

The waiting time seemed long, but it was only a few minutes. The nurse opened the entrance door and said, "Mary, please follow me. We are going to exam room 103."

Gale asked, "Is it okay if I go with her?"

"Yes, absolutely," replied the nurse. After arriving, the nurse said, "Please, sit on the exam table, and Doctor Kirk will be in shortly."

It was a matter of minutes before Doctor Kirk entered the room. He smiled while shaking hands with the two of them. He then said, "You must be the mother, Gale. Nice to meet you. And you, beautiful lady, must be Mary. I remember seeing you on the Ed Sullivan Show a while back. You were fantastic." His demeanor was reassuring, and his pink bow tie was an eye-catcher and relaxed everyone. He continued, "The larynx is often called the voice box. Its functions are phonating, swallowing, and breathing. The recovery time for a fractured larynx will vary depending on the severity of the fracture, the patient's overall health, and the treatment path we take. If we are lucky, and the problem isn't serious. You could be looking at four to six weeks of recovery time. It could be a few more weeks to several months if it is more serious. I plan on doing a tracheostomy/cricothyrotomy procedure, followed by a flexible laryngoscopy looking at the internal mucosal structures of the larynx and upper aerodigestive tracts. I will also be looking for any other structural abnormalities. If I discover any mucosal lacerations, I will do an endoscopic repair. All of what I have said depends on your approval. Do you have any questions, or have I thoroughly confused you?"

Mary spoke, "I haven't understood a word you have said. I have faith in you, though. Are all these normal procedures for my injury? How worried should I be?"

Doctor Kirk smiled and replied, "These tests are normal for your type of injury. I have studied the X-rays and other tests that have already been performed. I don't want to be premature, but I am confident we have a good chance for a positive outcome."

Mary looked at Gale, but said to the doctor, "I'm ready. You are easy to trust, and I know God will be with me."

The doctor motioned to his nurse, saying, "My nurse will take you to admissions. It would be best if you stayed in the hospital tonight. We will begin our medical procedures at sunrise. Try to get a good night's sleep, and we'll see you in the morning. Tomorrow will give us many answers, and maybe a solution we can perform." He bid them goodbye by bowing and exiting the room.

Mary was admitted to the hospital, and the nurses even made accommodations for Gale to stay with her. Both were impressed with Doctor Paul, and Gale knew Mary would receive excellent medical care. They were at peace with the proceedings scheduled for the next day.

Gale was so thankful as she said a silent prayer, thanking God for everything He was doing. She knew, in her soul, that Mary would be fine and return to her normal self. Gale called Lynn, relating the day's events and what the doctor had said. She felt good about the procedure.

Mary did too, but she was still very nervous. She asked, "Mom, is it okay to be nervous even though you know God will take care of you?"

"Yes, Mary," Gale replied. "That is only normal. Now, try to get some sleep because we have a big day ahead of us."

.

Chapter 26

SINGING

Mary, Gale, and Lynn enjoyed lunch at the Alamo Steakhouse in Caledonia, three weeks after their trip to Birmingham. It was Sunday morning, and following the church service, it was routine for them to eat at a local restaurant.

The examinations and ultimate surgery had been a resounding success. During the exam, Doctor Paul had seen the problem, which was bone fragments in the larynx. It turned out to be a simple procedure, but a not-so-simple surgery. His expertise made it less complicated than it could have been. He fixed the problem and corrected everything, so proper alignment was restored. The amazing part was that the hoarseness disappeared in less than two weeks, and she could sing. She was taking it slow at first, as her range gradually increased until she could hit all the notes she had sung before the injury.

Mary was sitting across the table from Gale and Lynn. She reached over and grabbed both their hands, held them tight, and said, "How can I say it, or what can I do to show my love for you? You both have done everything for me. You made sacrifices and commitments for me without me even asking. I have been through a lot these last several months, and you have been right by my side day and night. How can I ever repay you? I understand now what Mama Cossitt meant when she said, "Family stays together through thick and thin." Then Mary said, "I love you both and can't stop saying thank you, enough, from the bottom of my heart."

After a brief pause, with tears in her eyes, Gale said, "We love you too."

Mary began to cry as she looked down at the table and whispered, "I know a foundation paid for my operation and all the expenses, but who gave the money to them? I need to say a special thank you to them. If you know, please tell me."

Gale did not know what to say, so she shrugged her shoulders. "Maybe it was one of those God interventions and we're not supposed to know."

Mary then replied, "Why did all this happen to me? Mama Cossitt said God gave me an angel voice, then He took it away, and now, through His grace, it was restored. Is it wrong for me to ask why? What does it mean?"

Gale reached over, lifting Mary's face and wiping her tears. She looked into her eyes and said, "I believe that if God wants you to know the answers to your questions, somehow or somewhere you will learn them. In the book of Luke, your Bible says, 'giving is better than receiving'. Someone received a blessing by helping you with all that was medically needed to bring your voice back. God will reveal your answers in His time and place. Accept it and be thankful each day that you have a special gift for singing, and you should bless others with your voice and songs. Now, I suggest we order our food, and then plan on getting back in touch with Walter so you may share your gift."

Mary was in Walter's office the next morning. He was excited to see her and hear all about what had happened in Birmingham. They hugged and celebrated her return. Mary said, "I see you haven't changed a bit, and you are still chewing on those nasty old stogie cigars."

Walter laughed. "You're still the same old Mary, trying to change me from my bad and enjoyable habits."

"You bet I am, and I'll never stop," she said. In a different tone, she continued. "Thank you for what you've done for me and my career. You mentored me when I needed you the most, and I appreciate it more than you know."

Walter replied, "I should be the one thanking you. You showed me that I could do my job. I was able to take you to the top and promote your abilities. That was exciting and gratifying."

Mary continued, "That leads me to my band. How are the girls doing? What gigs do you have planned for them?"

Walter answered, "They are doing excellent, and the two singers performing with them are doing okay. They're not as great as you, but they are performing at a high level. As far as you are concerned, I would like you to sing individually, by doing some Nashville engagements. Your performances should gradually increase, leading up to more important venues as you go. Changing the subject, I need to ask you a favor if I may. My church has been praying for you every Sunday. Pastor Dale and his wife, Nancy, asked how you were progressing and wondered if you would perform two or more songs for them one Sunday morning. It would be like a fifth Sunday singing where the whole service is songs of God's love and grace. You can sing any songs you desire. Let the people know how much you appreciate their prayers. You can even ask the congregation to join in a church family singing. Be the choir director for a day."

Mary quickly answered, "I would be excited to do that, but only if you pick the date, so I have time off before then, and my voice isn't overworked."

Walter agreed, saying, "I will work it out to benefit you and the church."

Three weeks later, on the last Sunday of the month, Mary enjoyed the service with Pastor Dale and his congregation on a Sunday morning. Mary sang "Amazing Grace," "How Great Thou Art," and "Just as I Am," to name a few. She then asked the congregation to shout out their favorites so they could all sing them together. It became a blessing for the people in attendance and for Mary herself.

Walter showed up for the service, too. He had a great time. The people made him promise to bring Mary back again, or any of his other performers, for the next fifth Sunday sing.

Mary enjoyed the next few months feeling comfortable with her voice and its progress. She received many calls from people asking her to perform special music for them, and saying no to most of them was very hard. Everyone seemed to understand that she was trying to come back slowly from what most people considered a major throat operation. Mary wanted to follow Doctor Paul's instructions and not let anything get in her way.

There were days when Mary would, out of the blue, stop what she was doing and catch herself thinking about Kris. He had left an impressionable mark on her memory. Some of it wasn't pleasant, but the more she thought about him, the better times overcame them. She could not remove him from her mind. She tried to overcome it, but couldn't. He was an athlete who reminded her of sports she didn't enjoy. But he was a person who drew her mind toward him like a magnet. Mary thought of what Mama Cossitt would say, *Let the past be the past, live for today, and plan for tomorrow.* Mary knew that to see Kris again, she would have to go to him in Chicago or contact him directly, and she wasn't ready for that.

As Mary's voice, confidence, and performance improved, so did her commitments. Walter was doing an excellent job with her. During some of her engagements, Mary would see Gale and Lynn in the audience. They supported her as much as possible. She knew they had to live their own lives, but loved their support.

During a performance at a high-class establishment in Nashville, the Dream More Center. Mary had an unforgettable experience. This place had exceptional quality, catering to a discerning clientele and a privileged audience. She was singing country songs. Most people were on the dance floor, but one couple sitting at the table directly in front of the stage never danced. Mary observed that they would hold hands, touch their foreheads, and kiss. That left a lasting impression on Mary's mind of what true love is all about. After the show, Mary couldn't remove them from her thoughts. They didn't care who might be watching. They were about each other, not the music or dancing. This is what she wanted. If Kris were the person who would do that, she longed for it. The more she thought about everything, the more she was determined to find out. It was time for a break. She decided to fly to North Dakota, Minnesota, or wherever it took her, and confront Kris. She thought, *was he happy and still playing baseball? What if he had a girlfriend?* "It doesn't matter," Mary said out loud. "I'll start by calling Diane. She'll know."

Chapter 27

TRADED

Kris stood at second base in Minnesota's stadium on April 5th, 1970, for the opening day of the baseball season. He accomplished all his goals during spring training, realizing his ankle was as good as new. The stiffness and soreness had vanished. His ability to make sharp turns had returned, and his apprehension about another injury was gone. But most of all, his confidence was at an all-time high. He felt like he had a new lease on life.

The umpire yelled, "Play Ball!"

The first pitch by the Twins pitcher, Tom, was a called strike. The next two pitches were also strikes, except the batter had fouled the third one off, making the count no balls and two strikes. On the fourth pitch, the batter was ready. He swung as the fastball headed toward the outside edge of the strike zone for the right-handed batter. The bat and ball connected, sending it toward right field. Kris calmly watched the ball's trajectory, then jumped as high as he could, and caught the ball as it settled into the webbing of his glove. The first out of the new season, and he had accomplished it. It felt great. Kris knew this was an omen for a wonderful year to come. "I'm back, baby," he yelled as he threw the ball back to the pitcher.

The Twins had a fantastic start to the new season. After the first thirty games, their record was twenty-three wins and only seven losses. Their pitching had been outstanding, as they led the league with the fewest hits allowed, the fewest runs given up, and the lowest ERA. The five starting pitchers were having a season of personal bests. The team was scoring lots of runs to support them. Kris led the league again in batting average, runs scored, number of doubles and triples, and fewest errors committed. He was at the top of the world.

In life, things seem to happen that we have no control over. In the first game of a four-game series with the Los Angeles Dodgers, the Twins' number one pitcher made it into the third inning before tragedy struck. He threw a hanging curveball that the Dodgers batter swung at, connected on, and sent the ball well over the outfield fence for a long home run. Everyone was watching as the ball flew out of the park. Only the coach saw his pitcher grab his arm in pain. The coach and trainer rushed to the mound to check out his arm. The pitcher was done for the day. Unfortunately, they also found out later that he would be out for the rest of the season. He had hurt the medical epicondylar apophysitis. It is an overuse injury to the elbow caused by repetitive throwing. You get pain located on the inside part of the elbow. In 1970, this injury was commonly called the Little League Elbow. Surgical treatment included removing loose bodies, drilling to stimulate active repair, bone grafting when architectural support is needed, or reattachment with absorbable or nonabsorbable wires.

The second game of the series didn't go any better. A Dodger batter hit a line drive off the shin of their next starting pitcher, resulting in him being carried off the field on a stretcher. The result was a fracture of the fibula bone in the lower leg. Now, two starting pitchers were out for the season.

The team was relieved that nothing happened in the third game, but tragedy struck again during the fourth. In the seventh inning of a one-run game, the Dodger batter hit a towering pop-up in the infield between home and the pitcher. Immediately, the catcher called everyone off, saying, "I got it."

A gust of wind caught the ball, sending it backwards and to the side. The catcher lost his bearings, and as that happened, he lost the ball in the sun. At the same time, the third baseman and pitcher realized what was happening as they headed at full speed toward the ball. They collided, knocking each other out as the ball dropped between all three players. Both the third baseman and pitcher were taken off the field with concussions.

The team was now down three starting pitchers, and no one in the farm system was ready for the major leagues. They had to do something, or their season would become a disaster.

The Chicago Cubs saw what was happening and took advantage of the situation. They were willing to trade away two starting pitchers for an established second baseman. The Cubs' starting second baseman had been lost for the season due to a broken kneecap. They offered the Twins two pitchers and a boatload of cash for Kris.

The Twins were lucky in that they had another young second baseman in their farm system who was ready for the big leagues, and would cost them less money than Kris. They jumped on the deal, sending Kris to the Cubs.

Everyone was happy, except for Kris. To him, the Twins were a team that stuck together. How would he fit in with the Cubs? He had a lot of friends in Minnesota. His house was there. He would be a long way from Bob and Diane. It caught Kris by surprise. He was disgusted and felt unappreciated. A stab in the back wouldn't have hurt as badly as this.

Kris suddenly thought of Mary. He had heard from Diane that she was in Nashville singing again. She was happy and on top of the world, or so he was told. "Other players my age have families and enjoy life outside of baseball. I have no one. I've done this to myself," Kris said out loud. "I sure wish I'd have tried harder getting to know Mary. I hope she has forgiven me and not forgotten me. It's too late now, so I'd best make do with what's happened. I'm lonely. Please help me find that special someone you have for me."

Chapter 28

THE DECISION

Mary's scheduled commitment at the Dream More Center ended after her final performance on Sunday evening. Before calling Diane or Walter, she completed a few obligations before returning to her hotel room. She found the orchestra director as they were packing up all their instruments to head for a new location. "Thank you and all the orchestra members for doing a great job playing the music for me. All of you made my songs sound so much better. You're a terrific group, and someday I hope to be able to perform with you again."

They all smiled, and the director replied, "We had a wonderful time playing for you. Playing for a performer who can sing beautiful songs like you makes it fun. It would be our pleasure to play for you anytime."

Mary thanked them again, waved goodbye, and headed for the room Walter had reserved for her in the hotel. It was too late to call Diane tonight, so mentally she made plans for the following day. She would get up early and drive back to Caledonia, going straight to Walter's office. This would give her time to think about all the questions she needed to ask Diane and what she planned to tell Walter. Walter had done so much for her that she wanted him to know what she was thinking and planning for her future singing career.

The next day, as Mary drove through the beautiful countryside, it seemed to calm her emotions and clear her mind. She decided to call Diane from Walter's office. He had a right to listen to what was on her mind. She had to find out if her feelings for Kris were mutual.

Mary got Walter out of bed by calling him at 5:00 a.m. and telling him she was headed for his office. When she arrived, he was waiting and had many questions for her. Mary knew he would, but she needed to be honest with him. Walter was chewing on a stogie, alternating with sips of coffee and not looking too pleased.

Walter looked at her. "Who is Kris? he asked. "Have you talked about him before? Don't tell me, is he the one who hit the baseball?"

Mary answered, "Remember, I told you about the guy I met on the beach in Florida. He turned out to be Diane's friend from high school. And yes, he hit the baseball."

"So, you have forgiven him, am I correct?" asked Walter.

"Yes, I think I have. Before I agree to any more commitments, I need to know how this crazy baseball player feels about me. I've had mixed emotions, but deep down, I think he feels the same way I feel about him. I could easily love him. Does it sound stupid to think we are meant for each other?"

"No, it doesn't," said Walter. "But tell me. You are both talented in different fields. Are you ready to give up your talent and dreams for him?"

"I don't know," replied Mary. "But I want to find out."

"Well," said Walter, "Go for it then. I'll support you all the way. I'm here for you at any time. You are like a daughter to me, so all I want for you is happiness. Your career will always be here."

"May I call Diane from here?" Mary asked. "I want you to listen, and if you have any questions, please write them down."

Walter picked up a pen and paper, saying, "I'm ready."

Mary dialed Diane's number as Walter sat in a nearby chair listening. Diane answered on the second ring, saying, "Hello, church office. May I help you?"

"Diane, this is Mary. Do you have time to answer a few questions for me?"

"Hello, Mary." Diane said, "Why sure? What's on your mind? This sounds serious."

"Tell me about Kris. Have you heard from him lately? Is he dating anyone? Will you give me his phone number?"

"Hold on, Mary," said Diane. "Take a breath and tell me what this is about."

"This may sound crazy," Mary replied, "I'm not sure, but I may be in love with him. I have one question. Do you know who paid for my surgery?"

"I have no idea," replied Diane. "But it makes sense that Kris might have paid for it. I had never thought of that before."

"I watched a couple the other night while singing, and it made me think about Kris. He's said some things in our conversations that make me think he cares for me, but I've always run away. This couple brought those feelings back. Diane, what do you think? Does he like me?" Mary asked.

"I know he does," said Diane. "His phone number is 555-212-3456. And no, he's not dating anyone. Now you have his phone number, call him."

"Thank you, Diane. You have helped me with the information I need. I have to figure out what I'm going to do now. I'll be in touch. Bye for now," Mary said as she hung up the phone.

Walter spoke, "Mary, it sounds like you truly love this baseball player. You know that love is a two-way street, and the feelings must be the same for both people. Go and find this Kris guy and see if he feels the same way. But, be careful, I don't want you to get hurt. Also, it sounds like he may have been the person who paid for your surgery, but that can't influence your feelings for him. Love can't be bought. Mutual consent must be obtained between two people who care about each other. Paying for your surgery may be a true act of love, or it could be an act of guilt from within him. It's your responsibility to find that out. I believe faith will guide you."

Mary looked at Walter, saying, "My faith is not there, yet. I have always valued your comments, guidance, and judgment. What are your gut feelings about what you've learned?"

Walter got up from his chair and walked around the room for a minute, thinking. He stopped before her and said, "I've already told you to go. You need to call first and talk to him. Tell him you want to see him and ask if coming to Chicago is okay. If so, I can make your airplane and hotel reservations. When you meet him, ask him if he paid for your surgery. If he did, thank him because it had to be expensive. You must have faith and look to God for guidance because He is in control. He is just waiting for you to ask for His help."

Mary rose from her chair and kissed him on the cheek. She said, "To have a special friend like you is wonderful. You have done so much for me in the music industry, and now you go beyond that. You are family to me, as much as Mom and Lynn. I need to go and talk this over with them now. Thank you, you are the best."

Chapter 29

PHONE CALL

Kris was starting toward the front door when the phone rang. He had picked up his jacket and sports bag and was ready to leave for the stadium. Kris wanted to get in some early batting practice before the rest of the team arrived for their afternoon game. He continued walking toward the door, thinking whoever was on the other end would call back later. But something told him he needed to answer it. Kris put down his bag, rushed to the phone, and picked up the receiver, saying, "Hello, Kris speaking."

There was a slight pause, and then he heard her voice. "Kris, this is Mary. Do you have a few minutes to talk?"

Kris answered, "What a wonderful surprise. Yes, of course. How are you?"

"I'm fine," said Mary. "I just got home from a four-night performance in Nashville. I'm a little tired since I drove home early this morning, but I'm okay."

"It's sure great to hear from you. I've been thinking about you since North Dakota." Kris continued, "I hear your singing career has taken off again. I'm glad. I even watched a performance you gave in Nashville a few weeks back. You were outstanding."

"Thanks, but how did you see that? It wasn't broadcast," replied Mary.

"Sorry, I have a producer friend who got me a tape. I hope that doesn't upset you," said Kris. "I apologize if it does. I just wanted to see you and hear you sing."

"Not in the least," Mary replied. "It makes me happy that you are interested in seeing me. That is what I would like to talk to you about. Is it okay if I come to Chicago to see you?"

"Really? When? I can't wait," exclaimed Kris.

"But first, Kris, I need to ask you a question," Mary said. "This is something that I need to know, and please be honest with me. Do you know who paid for my surgery?"

Kris said while stuttering, "I thought a foundation paid for it. Does it matter?"

"It does to me," said Mary. "It was you, wasn't it?"

"I might have had a small part in getting it done. I wanted to see you happy and full of life like you were on the beach," replied Kris.

"So, you felt guilty for what had happened. Is that all?" asked Mary.

"No," said Kris. "I care about you more than you know. My guilt for what happened to you vanished when you told me you forgave me. I did this because I wanted to see you happy again. You deserve so much in life. Your talent is immeasurable. Seeing you sing again has brought me so much joy. Please don't get mad at me for that."

Mary took deep breaths and said, "I can't get mad at you. I truly thank you. How about if I come to Chicago this weekend? Is that good for you?"

"Yes, that would be great. I hope it's okay, but my parents are also coming this weekend. I would love you to meet them. I'm sure they would love to meet you, too. The Bud Billiken Parade and Picnic is this weekend. It's considered the second-largest parade in the United States," said Kris.

"If your parents are there, maybe I should wait until a better time. I don't want to be in the way," answered Mary.

"Not at all, Mary. I'd love for you to be here and meet them. The parade is about celebrating youth and education. It marks the end of summer vacation and the return to school for Chicago's youth. It's a 'back-to-school' celebration. We could enjoy it together."

"If you're sure, I think there's a flight into Chicago Friday evening around 9:30 p.m. I'll get a hotel and call you after I arrive," stated Mary.

"No, no, no," announced Kris. "I have three bedrooms in my house. I have plenty of room. You can stay at my house along with my parents. I will pick you up at the airport. Everything will be fine."

"Are you sure?" stated Mary.

"Absolutely. I wouldn't have it any other way," replied Kris.

"If you insist," said Mary. After an awkward pause, she continued, "Kris, I've been thinking about you, also. You do something to me and I can't explain it. All I know is that I want to find out more about you. I want to be with you, see what makes you happy and sad, and enjoy each other's company. Is that okay with you?"

"Mary, I feel the same way. I have for a long time. I think you are the most beautiful woman I have ever seen. You're talented and exciting, and I'm not afraid to say I think I love you."

Mary started to cry. Kris could barely hear her, but knew she said, "I feel the same way. I'll see you Friday."

As Mary hung up the phone, Gale stood next to her. They hugged for a long time. Then Gale said, "Are you sure about this young man? I'm proud of you, but please be careful. Your happiness is important to Lynn and me."

"Yes, Mom. Thank you for being here for me. I'm happy; very, very happy. I know my love for him is real."

"Well then, we best start planning what to pack," Gale said. "You have a big weekend in front of you."

Meanwhile, after hanging up the phone, Kris sat on the couch. He was in shock. His dreams were coming true. It seemed like a miracle to him. The longer he thought about her coming to Chicago, the more his mind raced, thinking about what they could do and where to go. He wanted to impress her. Eventually, thinking about her relaxed him as he sat there contemplating her arrival this weekend. It seemed like minutes, but the daydreams lasted for over an hour. Suddenly, he looked over at the clock on the wall, which instantly snapped him out of his dreams and brought him back to reality.

He would be late for the team meeting if he didn't hurry. His plan of being early to get in some extra work hadn't come to fruition, but he didn't care. This was the happiest day of his life.

Chapter 30

FATE

Kris's parents arrived the night before Mary was expected. They were excited when Kris told them about Mary and that she was coming for a visit the next day. They had been praying for Kris to meet the right woman and for him to be happy. Deep down, they desired grandchildren but would not say that out loud. Kris's mother was an elementary school teacher, so she was very excited about the parade that was happening on Saturday. She loved children and spent her whole life teaching them, loving them, and helping them to develop into fine young men and women. Her wish was for them to grow up and accomplish whatever they desired.

The Cubs' Friday afternoon ballgame against the San Diego Padres filled the ballpark with excited children celebrating their opportunity to attend the baseball game. Kris's parents got to sit in the first row behind the team's dugout, an area designated for the ballplayers' spouses and other family members.

Kris didn't disappoint his family as they saw an exciting game. The winning run was scored in the bottom of the ninth inning. Kris hit a double into the ivy wall in left field, resulting in his teammate easily scoring from second base to win the game. The opposing team's left fielder had trouble finding the ball in the ivy. It was Kris's tenth game-winning hit for the season. The Ivy Wall is unique for the Cubs' stadium because President Bill Veeck wanted to beautify his stadium by planting ivy on the outfield walls. It was English ivy at first, but was later changed to Boston ivy, which could endure the harsh Chicago winters better.

Kris and his parents celebrated winning the game by eating at the Wild Eagle restaurant, known for Chicago-style pizza and large chef salads. The best part of the meal was their dessert, an iconic Chicago Cake. Being a famous staple for the south side of the city, it's a layered cake built with one layer of banana topped with Bavarian custard, sliced bananas, and whipped cream; then one layer of chocolate cake topped with strawberry glaze, sliced strawberries, and whipped cream; then one layer of yellow cake topped with a layer of fudge icing; and the entire cake covered in whipped cream and fresh fruit.

Mary was to arrive at 9:23 p.m. at Chicago O'Hare airport. Kris thought it would be better if he went alone to pick her up, so he took his parents to his house, saying, "I'll be back as soon as I can. I know you both will love her."

After getting on Interstate 190 and heading west toward the airport, Kris was so excited he could hardly contain himself. Mary was coming to see him. He was also worried. "I hope everything goes right," he said out loud, talking to himself. "I've been looking forward to seeing her again for an eternity."

The traffic on the interstate seemed busier than normal. Kris glanced at his watch and saw that it was 8:45 p.m. He was thirty minutes from the airport. Figuring he had plenty of time to get there, there was no need to hurry. The eight-lane interstate was moving along at a constant speed, but a semi-truck up ahead seemed to be swerving back and forth. Kris figured that the driver was sleepy after a long haul from who knows where. The next twenty-three minutes passed with nothing exciting happening. The traffic was moving along at a constant pace with an occasional speeder shooting by on either side of his vehicle. As Kris realized the entrance and exit ramps to Interstate 294 were coming up, traffic slowed down. It's a notorious section of the interstate where many backups occur. He thought traffic to the airport would be easy once he got through this area. As he passed it, the traffic sped up to above-normal speed. "Great", he thought. Time to spare and be well-composed before he meets her.

Turning the next bend in the road, he saw the same semi again, but now it was driving erratically. Kris was now right on his tail. He wanted to get around him because the exit he needed to take was now less than one mile down the road, and the traffic on his right would make it very hard to move over. He sped up, and a gap opened between the truck on his right and a Camaro on his left. Going through the gap in his jeep was easy until the semi swerved to his left, entering his lane. Kris was three-fourths of the way by the Camaro when the semi hit Kris broadside between his door and right fender, sending Kris into the Camaro, and raising the jeep skyward toward the center concrete barrier. The jeep hit the top of the barrier, slinging it over into oncoming traffic. There was no time to react. Kris's jeep ran headfirst into the left side of a church van that had just dropped its youth group off at an outing one exit back. The crunch was loud and deadly. Both vehicles spun around and around as the jeep moved toward the center lanes of traffic, resulting in being hit broadside by another car, causing it to flip over two times. The van came to rest next to the concrete wall while Kris's jeep was on its top in the middle of Interstate 190, facing east in the opposite direction.

Chapter 31

ACTION

A young off-duty fireman passing by the wreck pulled over and immediately called 911. He hurried to check out both vehicles to see if he could help the people involved. The man in the church van only had a few scratches as the impact was more on the passenger side of his vehicle. He was struggling to get out when the fireman arrived to assist him. The driver was in shock, dazed, and very dizzy. The fireman sat him down against the center concrete barrier out of the way of any more danger, and said, "If you're okay, I need to check on the person in the jeep. Stay where you are and try to relax. Help is on the way."

Sirens could be heard as far away as the airport. Two firetrucks and an ambulance pulled up to the scene by the time the off-duty fireman got to Kris's Jeep. The hard-top Jeep was a crumbled mess. A paramedic reached his arm through the broken window, trying to get hold of Kris's wrist and check for a pulse. He shouted, "I got a pulse. He's alive, but he's very weak.

We need to get him out of the vehicle right away. Get the jaws of life equipment and let's get to work. He doesn't have much time."

The fireman who arrived on the scene first asked, "What can I do to help?"

The paramedic responded, "Help control the traffic and keep people away. We have limited time, so we must get this guy out of the Jeep as fast as possible. His life depends on it."

The firefighters and paramedics worked together to tear apart what was left of the Jeep. Working carefully to get Kris out without causing further damage was key. They used professional procedures as they removed his body from the entanglement. Once Kris was on the stretcher, they quickly loaded him into the ambulance. One paramedic tried to stabilize him because his blood pressure was dropping rapidly. The other paramedic checked on the van driver by the concrete wall.

The EMT in charge picked up his two-way radio with an encoder to contact Ascension Resurrection Hospital. It was set at frequency 155.340 MHz, the National HEARS (Hospital Emergency Alert Radio System) channel. He radioed the report to the hospital, "EMS 42 to Resurrection Hospital."

There was an instant reply on the other end, "Resurrection Hospital, go ahead 42."

"We are en route to your facility from just outside Chicago O'Hare Airport with a twenty-three-year-old male. From his license in his billfold, the patient's name is Kris Carlson, and his date of birth is 07-14-1947. The patient is unconscious, and BP is 80/55. It looks like he has multiple broken bones and could have internal bleeding. We are approximately six out. Any orders or questions?"

"42, no questions. Get here as soon as possible, CC2 upon arrival."

When the ambulance arrived at the hospital's emergency entrance, it was met by a six-person team of doctors and nurses. They hurriedly rolled Kris into trauma room number 1. As the doors closed behind him, there was a feeling of despair that hung over the room as the professional team of medical specialists went to work trying to save Kris's life.

Meanwhile, Mary's plane landed at Chicago O'Hare Airport. She was excited, but an odd feeling that something was about to go wrong hit her. She could not shake the feeling that something had happened. The airplane pulled up to the jet bridge, and people started to unload. Mary grabbed her pocketbook and carry-on bag from the overhead compartment and headed up the jetway into the airport.

Kris had told her to look for a sign saying Baggage Claim area and head that way. After arriving, she was to look for the door marked Concord 4, door 7, and he would be right outside to pick her up.

Mary didn't have a checked bag, so she proceeded directly to the spot where she was told, looking for Kris's bright red Jeep, which he had told her he would be driving. She exited door 7 and looked for his vehicle. She didn't see him, so she relaxed on the metal benches provided by the airport, thinking he would be there soon. Five minutes turned into ten, ten into twenty, and then twenty into forty. Mary was worried. Had he decided not to come?

Mary went back into the airport looking for a pay phone. She didn't know whether to call his house or call Diane. She decided on the latter because if his parents answered, she didn't know them, and she was sure there was a mix-up and he would be there shortly.

Diane answered, "Hello."

Mary said, "Diane, I'm at the airport in Chicago waiting for Kris, and he's fifty minutes late from when he told me he'd be here. I'm worried and don't know what to do. Will you help me?"

Diane said, "Sure. I'll call his house because his parents are there this weekend. They'll know what's happening."

Mary replied, "Thank you. Please call me back at 312-555-6574 when you find out something. I'm on a pay phone."

When Kris's mother answered the phone at Kris's house, Diane knew something was wrong. It sounded like mass confusion as Diane heard Kris's mother say, "We just got notified by Resurrection Hospital that Kris was in an accident. They found this phone number in his billfold. We're on our way to the hospital now. They didn't say how bad it was, but said to hurry. Gotta go."

Diane said, "I'll get hold of Mary."

As Diane dialed the phone number Mary had given her, panic set in. *What or how was I going to tell her what had happened?*

Mary answered the pay phone on the first ring, "Hello," not knowing who it was.

"Mary," Diane said. "Kris has been in an accident! His parents are on their way to Resurrection Hospital now. They were told to hurry. I'm sorry."

Mary replied, "I knew something was wrong. I'll grab a taxi and head there. You said it was Resurrection Hospital?"

"I think it's Ascension Resurrection Hospital," Diane said. "I don't think it's far from the airport. Call me when you find out something."

Mary didn't have time to get upset or even cry. She had to get to the hospital and find out what was happening. She hailed a taxi, jumped in, and shouted, "Resurrection Hospital, please hurry."

Chapter 32

HARD TO COMPREHEND

Mary and Kris's parents arrived at Resurrection Hospital about the same time. Mary had just asked the nurse at the information desk in the emergency department about Kris Carlson's condition as his parents walked up. They heard Kris's name and said, "You must be Mary. Have you found out anything about how Kris is doing?"

The nurse looked at all three and said, "Please tell me who's asking. How are you related and what's your name?"

Kris's mother answered. "Hi. I'm Janet, and this is my husband Frank, Kris's father.

Then Mary said, "I'm Mary, a friend of Kris's. How is he?"

The nurse looked at Frank and Janet and said, "I'm sorry, but I have no reports yet. All I can tell you is that he was in a serious car accident resulting in internal bleeding, broken bones, and a possible brain injury. The doctors are with him now, working to get him stabilized. Please have a seat in the waiting area, and as soon as I know anything, I will let you know. One of the doctors will probably be out to talk to you shortly."

Mary couldn't believe this was happening. She was in shock and complete denial and started to cry.

Kris's mom put her arm around Mary, hugging her tightly as they shed tears. The three of them moved to the waiting area and sat, stunned, in the corner of the emergency room. Janet said, "Mary, we're sorry to meet you like this. Kris has told us so much about you and was excited about your arrival tonight. He had plans to show you all over Chicago tomorrow after his ballgame. I could tell from talking to him that he truly cares and loves you."

"Mr. and Mrs. Carlson," replied Mary. "I love him too. I'm just sad, I've waited so long to tell him."

Janet continued, "Kris's father and I have prayed daily for him to find love in his life that will make him truly happy, and we believe that is you. Trust God, Mary. He will not leave us, no matter what happens."

Mary said, "I'm trying, but it's hard right now. I don't want to lose him."

"We don't either," said Frank, forcing back tears.

After three minutes of silence, Janet had had enough. "This is not doing us any good; we are just sitting here moping and thinking about the worst scenario. We need to be positive for Kris. Mary, tell us about yourself, your family, and what you like to do besides singing. Kris told us you have a fabulous voice and can bring the house down at your performances."

"Singing and playing the piano take up most of my life. I like to write songs, but haven't been very successful at it. I did win a contest a while back for a song I wrote. Performing on stage and making people happy brings so much joy to my life."

A man in a white coat walked out of the emergency department door. He looked at the three of them and said, "Are you the people here for Kris Carlson's family?"

The three were immediately on their feet, headed toward him. "Yes, we are," they said in unison. How is he?"

The doctor directed them to an empty room. After they entered, he said, "Please, have a seat and let me explain what we are facing. Kris has a leg broken in two places. He also has some internal bleeding, which we have identified and gotten under control, caused by some broken ribs. But the most damaging injury is a massive head injury from a blow he sustained in the crash. There is a brain bleed, but we don't know how severe yet."

Mary, trying to hold back tears, couldn't stand it any longer. She broke down into a continuous sob.

Kris's mother, Janet, hugged Mary as she asked with a weak voice, "When will we know something definite?"

"The next twenty-four to forty-eight hours will tell," said the doctor. We induced him into a coma to help his brain heal. A comatose brain needs less oxygen to function. This is helpful because blood vessels, compressed by increased pressure in the brain, can't supply brain cells with normal amounts of nutrients and oxygen. Monitoring twenty-four hours a day is necessary, watching for any worsening signs and pneumonia. I need to be honest with you, he probably has a twenty percent chance of surviving."

Kris's dad looked at the doctor as tears swelled in his eyes. "Thank you," he said. "Please keep us informed."

The doctor replied, "I know this is hard for everyone. If there is anyone else important in his life, they need to be contacted."

As the doctor said that, two men entered the room. The doctor recognized one of them as the Chicago Cubs manager. He was a man who cared a lot about his players. Kris's agent was undoubtedly the other. The doctor reiterated everything he had said to the Carlsons and Mary. Finally, he told everyone he was sorry but had to return to the ER.

The manager said, "If you need anything, please let me know. Kris is a great ballplayer, and I know in my heart he'll make it. He's strong and has a fighting heart. I'll be checking in on Kris and you often."

Mary located the closest payphone and called Diane and Bob. Diane had difficulty understanding everything Mary said because she was crying. Bob took away the phone and said, "We'll be on the next plane to Chicago. Get a hold of yourself, Mary. Diane and I will be there shortly."

* * * * * * * * * * * * * * *

By the next afternoon, Kris's condition worsened. Mary, Janet, Frank, Diane, and Bob were huddled outside Kris's hospital room as the doctors told them they didn't think he had much time left. Through the glass window, they could see on the blood pressure monitor that his blood pressure was steadily falling to a dangerous level. The EKG machine monitors the heart's electrical activity, which isn't in normal rhythm. As they watched, alarms started going off. The EKG machine showed a solid line. Kris's heart had stopped.

Mary grabbed Diane, crying, "This can't be happening. It's not right. Please, God, help him!"

They could see the doctors calling for the crash cart and the medical team going to work, trying to bring Kris back. They shocked his heart once, but it didn't work. "Again," shouted the doctor. "Let's do it again. Nurse, inject 1.0 cc of epinephrine. Everyone, stand back. Clear. I'm doing it now." The doctor shocked Kris's heart again. "Darn it, it didn't work. Resume cardiopulmonary resuscitation."

The doctors and nurses continued working for another twenty minutes, but to no avail. Finally, the doctor said, "Stop. Time of death is 9:33 p.m."

Mary couldn't take it. She pushed past the doctors and nurses on her way to Kris. She hit him with her fist hard on his chest a couple of times. "You can't leave me now. I love you and I need you!" she shouted. "Please come back to me." Mary lay her head on his chest with her arms hugging him as she began to cry.

All of a sudden, the EKG machine produced a beep. Then another beep. The doctors were in disbelief. Then another beep, and another. The heart started beating again. They pulled Mary off him and went back to work. The regular heart rhythm was returning.

Chapter 33

EPILOGUE

The sunset glowed a brilliant orange against the blue evening skies, looking west over Lake Sakakawea. Chairs covered in white cloth had been set up and directed toward a lighted cross facing the lake. People from all over the country filled the chairs to celebrate the union of a special man and woman.

It had been six months since the accident. Now, mostly healed but walking with a slight limp and cane, Kris stood at the front of the audience with Bob, his best man, next to him. To Kris's right was Michael, the preacher from the local church, performing the upcoming ceremony. Kris looked out over the crowd. He smiled as he recognized friends he had made from the Twins, the Cubs, and folks from the area where he had grown up. Many other people from the south were present and in awe of the beauty of North Dakota.

Kris looked over at his Mom and Dad sitting in the front row. He made a motion with his hands to show them his love. With his right finger, he pointed at himself, which meant 'I', then he crossed his arms over his chest, which meant 'love', and finally, he pointed his finger directly at his parents, which meant 'you'. Kris moved his lips, saying to them, "I love you." He then looked over at Mary's parents sitting in the front row on the other side, whispering, "Thank you."

The music started playing, coming from a full-sized organ brought in specifically for the occasion. A white cloth was laid down the center aisle, ready for the procession. The photographer moved to the top of the aisle as she aimed her camera toward the bridesmaids. Michael's wife, Ashley, was the first to appear and proceed down the white runner toward the front where Kris stood. She was followed shortly by Diane, who had the biggest and brightest smile, as she walked down the aisle toward the two most important men in her life. The odd plus-one threesome was about to add a fourth person to their group. Then came a nephew and niece. The niece spread rose petals on the white runway as she descended the aisle. The nephew carried a white pillow containing rings tied to it, signifying the marriage of Mary and Kris.

The organist began to play the Bridal Chorus, commonly known as "Here Comes the Bride". The entire audience stood and looked toward the back of the outdoor assembly. Kris's eyes focused on the entrance of a beautiful woman dressed in an elegant wedding dress as she started down the walkway. Mary was the most wonderful woman he had ever met. The doctors told him she saved his life. Mary told him it was not she, but God, that brought him back as she hugged him and prayed for his recovery. God intervened and started him breathing again.

Mary, escorted by Walter, proceeded toward the front. Tears formed in Kris's eyes. How could I have been so blessed? Kris thought to himself. "This woman not only saved my life but also did not leave my side following the accident. Mary supported me through all the pain and anguish, dressed my wounds, and encouraged me constantly during both the tough and easy days of therapy aimed at healing my body. She never once complained or thought about her professional career."

As Mary approached Kris, they reached out for each other. Diane took the bouquet from Mary, and Walter let her hands go to Kris's. Mary and Kris turned toward Pastor Michael, and Diane straightened Mary's dress, which flowed outward for at least fifteen feet.

Pastor Michael began the wedding ceremony by greeting all those in attendance. He said," Who gives this woman to marry this man?"

In unison, Gale, Lynn, and Walter stood and said, "We do." Everyone in the crowd cheered as the three sat in the chairs at the front.

Their vows to each other were repeated in their own words. There was only one slight glitch. Mary had trouble saying what she wanted because tears of joy got in the way. Kris helped her through it by squeezing her hands with assurance as they looked into each other's eyes. The rings were then exchanged, signifying their love for each other.

After gaining her composure, Mary entertained the crowd by singing, "I Wanna Dance with Somebody (Who Loves Me)", written by George Merrill and Shannon Rubicam, and made popular by Whitney Houston. Mary dedicated the song to Kris.

In a move to profess their faith in God, Mary and Kris lit three candles symbolizing God as the head of their family because He had made their union possible. Finally, they turned to face the audience as Pastor Michael said, "It is my pleasure to present Mr. and Mrs. Kris Carlson. God has blessed this day. This is a day When Happiness Came Down From Heaven."

About the Authors

CURT YOUNG

Curt Young spent his high school years in the small town of Caledonia, Mississippi, where he discovered and nurtured his passion for music. During this time, he developed a deep love for playing the guitar, often dedicating countless hours to practice and improve his skills. He also enjoyed the creative process of writing music, allowing him to express his thoughts and feelings through his art.

His talent did not go unnoticed, as he earned first place in a prestigious talent contest held at his school. This significant achievement was not just a personal victory; it opened the door to numerous opportunities for him to showcase his musical abilities. As a result, he found himself performing in a local musical band, collaborating with fellow musicians, and gaining invaluable experience in the vibrant world of music that he loved so much.

After high school, he attended college earning a degree in marketing and business management. He served in the military and married his college sweetheart. He worked for a national pharmaceutical company and retired to the State of Tennessee. He purchased a small farm and went back to his farm days of raising farm animals and remembering the good days when happiness came down from Heaven.

Frank S. Snyder, DPh.

Frank Snyder is a Doctor of Pharmacy in Tennessee, a North Dakota State University College of Pharmacy graduate, and a husband to my loving wife, Vickie. I am a father of two wonderful girls, Ashley and Cynthia, and a papaw to my loving grandchildren. Currently serving as chairman of the Rhea County Election Commission and board member for 6 years. An active member of the Authors Guild of Tennessee in Knoxville. I'm a retired pharmacist of 45 years and owned my own business for 29 years. I'm proud to be a long-time member of the Tennessee Pharmacist Association, a member of the Spring City Methodist Church, and a former board member of the Rhea Medical Center Board of Directors. I also served on the Spring City Chamber of Commerce Board of Directors and member while owning my business, Spring City Pharmacy Inc. After retirement, I enjoy writing books with my best friend, playing golf, looking for antiques, and collecting gems stones, and rocks of every color and size. Traveling to Arizona in the winter months has been a blessing and a long-time dream come true.

In life, one of my proudest achievements has been serving on short-term Medical Mission teams helping patients in Mexico, for 16 years, Haiti for 2 years, Guatemala for 6 years, and Nicaragua for 1 year.

I encourage everyone to stay active after retirement and enjoy the beauty that God has given us. My friend and I use our daily motto, "Walk or run to exercise your body. Read to exercise your mind."

www.ingramcontent.com/pod-product-compliance
Lightning Source LLC
Chambersburg PA
CBHW070513260626

47161CB00004B/1540